It was the killer. . . .

I crept across the roof to the back edge. I looked down. It wasn't too far to the ground. I swung my legs over the side, letting myself slip slowly over the edge until I was hanging by my hands, only a foot above the ground. Then I dropped.

I dropped all the way to my hands and knees. I planned to head toward town, cutting through yards. As soon as I found a house with a light on, I'd go in and call the police. Just a little while longer, and I'd be safe.

It was almost completely dark by now, which would help me hide. I was struggling back to my feet when I froze.

Something cold touched the back of my neck. It was a gun. I closed my eyes as a hateful voice asked, "Leaving so soon?"

It was the killer.

Read these terrifying thrillers
from HarperPaperbacks!

Babysitter's Nightmare
Sweet Dreams
Sweetheart
Teen Idol
by Kate Daniel

And look for

Class Trip
by Bebe Faas Rice

The **Nightmare Inn** series
#1 *Nightmare Inn*
#2 *Room 13*
#3 *The Pool*
#4 *The Attic**
by T. S. Rue

* coming soon

RUNNING SCARED

KATE DANIEL

HarperPaperbacks
A Division of HarperCollins*Publishers*

This is a work of fiction. The characters, incidents, and dialogues are products of the author's imagination and are not to be construed as real. Any resemblance to actual events or persons, living or dead, is entirely coincidental.

HarperPaperbacks *A Division of* HarperCollins*Publishers*
10 East 53rd Street, New York, N.Y. 10022

Copyright © 1993 by Daniel Weiss Associates, Inc. and Kate Daniel
Cover art copyright © 1993 Daniel Weiss Associates, Inc.

All rights reserved. No part of this book may be used or reproduced in any manner whatsoever without written permission of the publisher, except in the case of brief quotations embodied in critical articles and reviews. For information address Daniel Weiss Associates, Inc., 33 West 17th Street, New York, New York 10011.

Produced by Daniel Weiss Associates, Inc., 33 West 17th Street, New York, New York 10011.

First printing: August, 1993

Printed in the United States of America

HarperPaperbacks and colophon are trademarks of HarperCollins*Publishers*

10 9 8 7 6 5 4 3 2 1

For my mother,
Nellie Marie Morgan.
Thanks, Mom.

~ One ~

I'm not sure what made me look up just then. But I did, and I saw him. Mr. Dillman, my mom's former boss, stood at the cash register signing a credit-card slip. At that moment I realized that coming to Chicago had been the worst mistake I'd ever made in my life—and it might be the last one.

I froze, then whipped my head around, facing away from him. It *was* him; I was sure of it. A look of terror must have flashed across my face, because Miss Ahrens asked me what was wrong.

"Nothing, I just feel—where's the bathroom?" I spotted the sign. "Never mind. See you in a second." I hurried toward the rest rooms at the far end of the restaurant. My back felt hot, as if Mr. Dillman were staring at me. When I got

1

to the bathroom, I locked myself in and started shaking. I stayed in there for at least ten minutes before I heard a knock on the door.

"Donna?" It was my friend Tina. "Donna, are you all right?"

"Yeah, my stomach's a little jumpy. Stage fright, I guess. I'll be out in a couple minutes."

It was a convenient excuse. I really was afraid, but it had nothing to do with the play we were supposed to put on in a few hours. Leaving the shelter of the locked door took all my willpower. I expected to see Mr. Dillman staring at me, but an old man was at the cash register instead. My mom's ex-boss was nowhere in sight.

As we walked back to the school that was hosting the play contest, I almost went cross-eyed looking every direction at once, but I didn't see Mr. Dillman again. By the time we were inside, I started to wonder if it really had been him. It had *looked* like him. Tall, with a dark complexion, silvery-gray hair, and a dark bristly mustache. But there were probably a lot of men who fit that description, and I did only catch a glimpse of the man at the cash register. Maybe it wasn't Mr. Dillman after all.

We weren't scheduled to perform until late in the contest, so our whole group found seats to watch the other plays. My boyfriend Greg sat next to me and draped his arm around my shoulders. It felt good there, and I needed the comfort. He handed me a program, and I sat there flipping through the pages while I waited for the houselights to dim. Just before the first play began, I found the cast list for Norwell High. There I was, Donna White as Abby Brewster. But there was one problem with the listing.

My name isn't Donna White. It's Donna Aubrey.

Greg played the lead and was the assistant director of *Arsenic and Old Lace*, the play we were performing. He wants to be a professional actor, and I'm positive he'll make it someday. His good looks are only part of why I'm so sure. Greg is incredibly handsome, but he's such a talented actor, he can convince you he's a complete dork. And he can come across as if he flunked Stupid School, even though he's one of the smartest guys I know.

Dating Greg and being in the play were the best things that had happened to me since we'd moved a few months before. We got there just after the start of the second semester of my senior year. At first it had been hard to make friends. I had a new name and a new, made-up history, and I felt like a liar every time I opened my mouth. I couldn't talk about anything that went on in my life before moving to Norwell, so I kept my mouth shut.

After a few weeks, though, I started to relax a little. Once I met Tina Cottingham, things became easier for me. Tina has about a million friends, and through her I met most of the senior class. Then she introduced me to Greg.

That day I had been eating lunch by myself, wondering why school spaghetti was as gross in Illinois as it was in Pennsylvania, when I heard Tina call my name. I looked over my shoulder. She was standing there holding a tray, and there was a guy with her. I'd seen him around school already—Greg Florian stood out. Straight dark hair, dark eyes, and a smile that almost *glowed*.

"You look like you need company," Tina announced. She slid into the seat across from me, leaving the one next to me for Greg. "Greg, this is the new girl I was telling you about," Tina said. "Isn't that a bummer, having to transfer in your last semester? Donna, this is Greg Florian."

I mumbled something into my spaghetti sauce. I was getting used to my new name, but I still felt shy about meeting people. I'd never been shy before.

"Hi," he said. His voice was a perfect match for his smile, warm and alive. "Yeah, I'd really be ticked off if I had to move right before graduation. But Donna's lucky. She got to come *here*." He grinned at me.

4

"Maybe you guys are the lucky ones. You get to *have* me here," I said, grinning back at him. Tina and Greg were both so nice that I felt my shyness disappear.

"So how'd we get so lucky?" he asked.

"My mom got a new job, so we had to pack our bags," I said with a shrug.

"Bummer," Greg said, echoing Tina. "So anyway, you into sports or anything? What do you like to do when you're not eating lousy spaghetti?"

"Nothing much." That sounded stupid, so I tried again. "I read a lot. Listen to music. That's about it, I guess." I didn't mention the French Club or Chess Club. That had been part of Donna Aubrey's life.

His dark eyes intent on me, he asked, "How'd you like to be in the senior class play?"

"I've never acted," I told him.

"Neither have most of the kids who'll be auditioning," he said. "Look, the worst thing that can happen is you don't get a part."

"No, the *worst* that can happen is I'll look like an idiot."

"Only if it's in the script," he said. He smiled at me, and I felt myself smiling back in spite of myself. "And that isn't fatal. Besides, you'll be great, I know it."

Somehow I doubted that. But Greg was per-

5

suasive, and before lunch was over, I had promised to show up after school on the following Tuesday. It sounded like fun, and it was something completely new for me. By the time I had gotten home, I'd been really excited about the play. It was the first thing I'd been enthusiastic about in months.

The lights in the auditorium came up, and I stopped daydreaming about what had happened three months before. It was time for us to get ready. I was eager to get into my costume and makeup; in fact, I wished I'd been in it at lunch. In the play I wore a flowery dress down to my ankles and a white wig and a ton of stage makeup. I looked about fifty years older than my grandmother, and when I saw myself in the mirror, I could barely recognize the person gazing back at me. Once I got into character, I'd be safe if Mr. Dillman walked in and saw the play. There was no reason for him to watch a high-school drama contest, but when you're as anxious as I was, little things like common sense don't matter.

"Scared?" Greg asked, while we waited for our signal to take the stage. I nodded. It was the truth, but it had nothing to do with normal stage fright. "Don't be. You'll be great."

"Yeah, right," I said. I tried to joke around, but my heart wasn't in it. All I could think about was Mr. Dillman.

"Hey, lighten up," Greg said. "You're the best. As an actor and as a girlfriend." He leaned over and kissed my ear, which was the only place he wouldn't get a mouthful of makeup.

"I'm still scared," I said. We sat there quietly holding hands, while I tried to think about the play. I didn't succeed, but that's not surprising. It's hard to worry about things like contests when at any second you may have to run for your life.

Running for our lives was how Mom and I had wound up in Norwell. Mom had turned Mr. Dillman in to the Lakewood Heights police and then had been the star witness against him in a criminal racketeering trial. Gangsters, organized crime—none of it had seemed real to me at first. The trial dragged on for weeks, but I was more concerned about missing school and the senior class trip than anything else. I had looked forward to the end of the trial, since I figured life would get back to normal then. Of course, I knew Mom would need a new job, since I expected Mr. Dillman to go to prison, but that didn't seem like such a big problem.

The jury was out for days. Finally they came back and said they couldn't agree, and since a verdict must be unanimous, the judge declared a mistrial. That's when the district attorney told

Mom about the Federal Witness Security Program.

It sounded grim. The program was designed to protect witnesses the government was afraid might be murdered. The witnesses and their families were given a phony history and moved to a new place with new names and a chance to start a whole new life. But going into the program would mean that Donna Aubrey wouldn't exist anymore. You weren't even supposed to write letters to old friends, and you couldn't tell anyone what was going on. Sometimes witnesses came out of the program when the danger was past. But most of the time, they were in for life.

The program is run by the Marshal Service. I'd always thought U.S. marshals were something in old cowboy movies, but they still exist. We met our contact, a man named Marris, and he gave us our "cover story." They changed everything about us. Dad died when I was fourteen, in a plane crash, but the cover story said Mom had gotten a divorce when I was a little kid. She has a degree in accounting, but the jobs they found for her were just simple bookkeeping ones. It was like some fairy godmother in reverse had waved a black magic wand. Because Mom had tried to be a good citizen, we weren't going to be ourselves anymore.

They even made us change the way we

looked, or at least our hairstyles. It took me almost as long to get used to the new hairdo as it did to get used to my new name. I had to dye my hair several shades darker than my natural light brown and then cut it short, about four inches long on top, with the back clipped close. At least it was easy to take care of.

They gave Mom a choice of three different jobs, none of them very good, and she picked the one in Norwell. But that was the only decision they let us make. Until I met Tina and Greg, I felt lost. Everything in the past was off-limits. I couldn't join the Norwell French Club, since I had so many memories of my old French Club that could trip me up. I couldn't talk about going to Montreal with the club last summer. I couldn't tell my friends about Madame Labrouste, who was French and went back to Paris every summer. The photos she'd given me of the Cathedral of Notre Dame had been left behind with my Pearl Jam posters, Mom's record collection, and most of our other stuff.

I finally started to fit in once play rehearsals began. Donna White wasn't just a part anymore, it was me. Mom was glad that I was happy. I think she'd been more worried about me than about herself. She knew I had resisted going into the program.

What she didn't know was why I'd agreed to

take on a new identity. I knew we didn't have any choice but to run.

If we stayed in Lakewood Heights, we would both be killed.

When Mom first told me about the program, after the trial, I really hated the idea. I didn't like the guy from the District Attorney's office who explained it all to me, and I couldn't believe the things he was talking about. Gangsters, murder, our lives being in danger—all that sort of thing was like something on TV. It didn't have anything to do with me, with a high school senior who liked French and math.

Then I ran into Sheri, the secretary at Dillman Brothers. When the trouble started, they had padlocked the place. Mom hadn't been back. Sheri told me Mr. Dillman had torn Mom's office apart looking for a tape recorder. There wasn't one there, but Sheri said he was so mad, he ripped things apart anyway. She'd gone in afterward and packed up all of Mom's personal stuff that Mr. Dillman hadn't wrecked. It was still sitting there in a box, as far as she knew. Most of it was junk, but I knew Mom would want some of it back. And there was one photo I wanted, a picture of me with my father, taken when I was ten. If we went into the program, we might have to leave it behind, but I still didn't want to leave it there.

I figured Dillman's would be deserted, but I was careful anyway. I didn't go near the pad-locked front gate. There was a place around back near the railroad tracks where the ground had washed away years before. The bottom of the chain-link fence was more than two feet above the ground at one point. I wiggled under and headed for the beat-up trailer that had been Mom's office. I had Mom's old key, so I thought I could just grab the stuff and leave. It would be embarrassing if they caught me, but that was all. Mr. Dillman was a crook, sure, but even after everything that had been said, I couldn't believe we were in real danger.

Not until I saw Harry Leiberwitz backed up against the wall of the main building. He was a reporter who'd interviewed Mom about the case, and he'd been writing stories about Mr. Dillman's criminal connections. The stories traced how many millions of dollars Dillman's had handled, hinted about something called "money laundering," mentioned government people who might have been taking bribes. It was the biggest thing ever to hit Lakewood Heights, and if half of the stories were right, it reached a lot farther than our suburban town.

I stepped out between two rows of big rusty barrels and saw Harry facing a couple of men.

One of them had his back to me, but I could see the other one's face. I didn't recognize him. I started to say something, then Harry's eyes caught mine and he moved his head just a little. I froze. Something was wrong. One of the men was pointing something at Harry. It was a gun.

People talk about time standing still, but it didn't. And there wasn't any sudden silence, as there always is in the movies. The traffic on Route 276 was heavy with trucks, and someone was leaning on a horn. I could hear it, but it didn't seem to have anything to do with me or Harry or the man with the gun.

An instant later the gun went off. I'd been trying to forget that moment ever since, but it kept repeating in my bad dreams. It was as if someone had thrown Harry back against the side of the building, hard. I saw his face for only that one second, but I doubt if I'll ever forget it. He looked more surprised than anything else.

I ran. I don't know why I didn't scream. I just sprinted away, terrified and feeling sick. I must have made some noise, because I heard the killers shout something. One good thing about a big yard full of trucks and heavy equipment and oil drums: there are lots of places to hide. If I ever have kids, one game they won't get me to play is hide-and-seek. I don't know how long I played it that day, but it seemed like hours.

Finally I got close to the place where I'd crawled under the fence. I waited until I could hear the men over on the other side of the yard, then I rolled under the fence and ran to my car.

When I got home, I threw up until my sides ached, and cried until I could hardly see, my eyes were so swollen. When Mom got home, though, all I told her was that I was upset about leaving Lakewood Heights. The next day we vanished into the program. I never told Mom or the marshals what I'd seen. I was afraid to. If I'd told the police, there would have been delays while they questioned me, and Mom wanted to get into the program as fast as possible. Besides, she was scared anyway. If she knew I'd witnessed a *murder*, she would have been too terrified to breathe.

So no one knew I was an eyewitness to murder, except the murderers. But what had me shaking as I sat there in the green room, holding Greg's hand and waiting to go onstage, was the memory of seeing Mr. Dillman at the restaurant.

I hadn't wanted to leave Lakewood Heights in the first place, but Norwell was home now, and I was happy being Donna White. If Mr. Dillman had seen me, we'd have to go on the run again. And this time we might not get away.

~ Two ~

Miss Ahrens clapped her hands for attention. "All right, people, let's go. Break a leg!"

Greg gave me a quick hug; then we made our way up the stairs onto the stage, finding our places in the dim work lights. I tried to focus on my lines, but I kept seeing Mr. Dillman in my imagination. The contest had made me nervous from the first day I heard about it. Inspector Marris still didn't know I was in a play, let alone a competition in Chicago. There's no way he would have let me leave Norwell; the town was the only safe place for Mom and me to be. It didn't make me feel any better to realize that Inspector Marris would have been right. I never should have come to Chicago.

The fight with Mom when I told her about

the contest was one of the worst we'd ever had. What finally convinced her to let me go ahead was my costume. We'd had one dress rehearsal, with full makeup, and Tina had taken Polaroid pictures of us all. I hadn't wanted mine taken, since one of the rules of the program was *No photos!* But I finally decided that one Polaroid shot was probably harmless, especially since I got to keep it. I showed it to Mom, and she admitted that she wouldn't recognize me in that getup. The wig was the best part of my costume. Tina's hair was long enough that she just put it up in a bun and sprayed it gray, but I had a professional theatrical wig. Mom and I agreed we wouldn't tell Inspector Marris about the contest. It was a million to one that anyone would see me, and a trillion to one that they'd recognize me even if they did. I never even considered the possibility of someone seeing me *offstage* without makeup. I guess long shots happen sometimes.

I had almost dropped out anyway a few weeks after we started rehearsal. We got a call from Inspector Marris one night. We hadn't expected it, since we hardly ever heard from him. That was another of the program's rules: *Minimum contact.* The whole idea of the program is to make a new life, and it's hard to do that when you have U.S. marshals hanging around.

As usual he wouldn't tell me anything. He insisted on talking to Mom. When she hung up, she just stood there, biting her lip.

"Mom?"

"They wanted to make sure we hadn't contacted anyone back home—back in Lakewood Heights," she said. "They think there's been a murder connected with the case. Remember that reporter who interviewed me? Harry Leiberwitz?"

I nodded. Of course I remembered Harry—I dreamed of his death almost every night. But I still couldn't tell Mom what I'd seen happen that horrible day.

"He vanished about the same time we did," she went on. "I didn't tell you, because I didn't want you to worry." She closed her eyes for a moment. When she opened them, it looked as if she was about to cry. "They found his body, and they think his death is connected with the Dillman case."

There hadn't been anything to say. I wanted to tell her that I *knew* Harry's murder was connected to Mr. Dillman, but I couldn't. If I told Mom that I was a witness to a killing, she'd practically die worrying about me. And the program would certainly make us move again; we'd never have lives of our own.

The next afternoon at rehearsal, while I was setting up the props we used onstage, an image

17

of Harry flashed in front of me—an image of a man who was drawing his last breath. I dropped a decanter I'd been filling, and the black-cherry Kool-Aid we used for poisoned wine went all over. I had to leave rehearsal before I got sick.

I hadn't been able to explain why I was upset, even to Mom. The next couple of days I spent home in bed, pretending to have the flu. I had finally decided that dropping out of the play wouldn't help Harry any. But somehow it still felt wrong.

And now it felt not only wrong but *stupid*. Stupid to have risked my mother's life and my own just to be in a play. But the curtain was opening, and it was too late to back out.

I don't remember much about the actual performance, though a few things do stand out in my memory. At one point Tina forgot her lines, and I was able to pick them up before there was a dead spot. Greg was fantastic, as usual. But I can't recall much about saying my lines. When the audience started to applaud at the end of the act, I realized we'd finished.

I didn't care if we'd won the contest or not; I just wanted to get on the bus and start the three-hour drive back to Norwell. But until the competition was over, we had to sit in the auditorium watching the other schools' performances. Tina went to take off her makeup, but I left mine on. When we were safely back in Norwell, and I'd locked myself in my bedroom, then I'd take my wig and makeup off.

I have no idea what plays the other schools did. Instead of watching, I sat there trying to figure out what to do next. If I told Inspector Marris, we'd be removed from Norwell in a flash, disappearing into the program with another new identity. If I told Mom, she'd definitely tell Marris. I liked Norwell, and I didn't want to move again. And there was Greg—I really cared about him and wasn't ready to say good-bye. Besides, in less than a month I was supposed to graduate. If we moved, I might never graduate from high school. The program would fix me up with a diploma, a real one since I'd done the work, but it wouldn't be the same thing.

It was like telling Mom about Harry Leiberwitz. If I did, she'd be scared and it wouldn't really help anything. If I didn't, well, nothing would probably happen, and I didn't even want to think about what might happen if something did. Part of me knew it was the right thing to do and wanted to tell her. But another part of me—the part that needed to be a normal high school student more than anything—didn't.

I didn't even hear the judge announce, "Norwell High." The rest of the cast did, though. We'd won the contest, and everyone was going crazy celebrating.

For the first time all day, I forgot about Mr. Dillman. We all went up onstage, and the judges handed Greg the prize. He was so happy and excited, he kissed me right in front of all those people. I was grinning when a camera flash went off, and I froze. Tina's Polaroid had been okay. There was only one copy, and I had held on to it. But even with my makeup and wig, someone could recognize me in a photograph. I felt a chill run through me as I realized what was happening.

The camera flashed again, but by that time I had my face buried in Greg's chest. He pushed me away slightly, trying to get me in position for a good picture, but I turned my head to the right, so all that showed was the back of my wig.

"Donna!" he urged without losing his smile or moving his lips. "Smile!" He nudged me again as another flash went off. This one was from closer to the right, and I turned slightly so I was looking upstage.

"I don't like having my picture taken," I said. It had been a day for understatements.

"Turn *around*," he muttered. He tugged at my arm again. Tina was on my other side by now, her arm around me, and I could feel her nudging me as well.

I didn't want to draw any more attention to myself, so I turned around, but instead of facing the camera, I ducked my head. I was wearing old-fashioned clunky black heels with laces, old-lady shoes, and I stared down at the rounded toes. There was more applause, a few more camera flashes, and then we left the stage as the judges went on to announce the rest of the prizes.

Greg scowled at me.

"What was *that* all about?" he asked.

"I told you, I hate having my picture taken."

"Come on, Donna, get real." Tina was on the other side of Greg, and she leaned forward as she spoke. "A lot of people don't like it, but they don't act like that! Especially not when they're getting an award."

"It's just the way I am," I said.

I knew everyone was puzzled by the way I'd acted, and I honestly couldn't blame them. I also couldn't explain my odd behavior, so it meant the trip back would be a long one. I didn't care, though, as long as I could get out of Chicago.

As long as I could make it back to Norwell.

As it turned out, I didn't have any choice

whether or not to tell Mom about the photographers. The Chicago newspaper printed a story the next day about the contest, listing the schools and the winners, with a picture. It must have been the first one taken, because you could see my face. Even with the makeup and wig, it looked like me.

Mom was so upset, I didn't even try to tell her about seeing Mr. Dillman. I hoped she hadn't seen an article that was on the front page. Before his death Harry Leiberwitz had hinted that a government official had been taking bribes. The FBI must have been following his leads, because they'd arrested a man in Chicago. There was a picture of the man and Mr. Dillman. The caption called the guy a "major figure in organized crime."

Mr. Dillman had probably been in Chicago to see him. If the article was right, there'd be several more trials, and they might take years. Mom was just a witness in the Dillman's case, but if they could get him, they'd be able to go after all the others. But first they had to convict Mr. Dillman. Mom was the key witness, so we were in worse danger than ever.

I guess that's why I got so angry when Greg came over that afternoon. We'd gotten back late, and even though I'd slept until almost noon, I was still tired. As soon as I was up, Mom had jumped me about the picture. I think she felt guilty about letting me go to Chicago at all, which made her even madder at me. The argument ended with Mom walking out of the apartment and slamming the door.

A few minutes later I found the article about Mr. Dillman, and I knew I hadn't imagined seeing him the day before. I looked at the picture of me and the rest of the cast again. The costume and makeup wouldn't fool anyone, I decided. Even if he hadn't seen me in the restaurant, he'd see me in the paper.

Mom was right—I'd been a selfish idiot even to think about being in the play. We'd have to move, probably within the next day or so. I was crying and wishing Mom would get home so we could pack, when Greg showed up.

"Hey, what's wrong?" he asked.

"Nothing," I said. I tried to wipe my eyes without being too obvious, then decided he'd seen the tears already. I went into the bathroom to blow my nose and wash my face. When I came out, Greg was looking around the apartment as though he'd never seen it before.

"Sorry," I told him. "I'm feeling kind of depressed. I guess it's just the letdown after the contest or something."

"You really are afraid of cameras, aren't you?" he asked, still looking around.

23

I knew what he was seeing, or rather what he *wasn't* seeing. Most homes have at least a few photos around. We'd had photos and paintings and drawings all over our house in Lakewood Heights. Pictures of the family, copies of famous paintings Mom loved, some sketches and paintings Dad had done. All of them had been put in storage, in case we ever got out of the program. Now, even after living here for four months, the apartment walls were bare.

"You and your mom both," Greg said. He turned to face me. "I never thought about it before, but I don't think I've ever seen a picture of either one of you."

"Yeah, I guess we have a phobia about it or something," I said. I tried to make it sound like a joke. "I should have warned you."

"I haven't ever seen *anyone* that camera shy." He picked up the paper, which was lying there on the end of the couch. "For a newspaper photo, this isn't too bad."

"I don't like it," I said.

"Wait, I *have* seen one picture of you. You didn't mind when Tina took pictures during the first costume rehearsal." His eyes narrowed. "So why does this one bother you so much?"

"Those were Polaroids."

"What difference does *that* make?"

There was no way I could explain why

24

Polaroid pictures were safe. Meanwhile, I didn't know for sure if we were going to have to move again. Greg was part of the reason I didn't want to leave Norwell. It was all so weird. I was getting mad at Greg because I might have to leave him behind over that stupid picture, and he liked the thing.

Mom got home then, which was lucky, or I might have spilled everything to Greg. That shook me up, realizing how badly I wanted to tell him. I had thought I was over the need to confide in someone, but that afternoon it was as bad as it had been during the first few weeks after we started dating. I understood at that moment that our whole relationship was based on a lie.

Even worse, I didn't know if I'd ever have the chance to tell Greg the truth.

I was jumpy and moody for the next few days, and so was Mom. School didn't help. Winning a play competition isn't as big a deal as making the state basketball play-off, but it was still a win for Norwell, and we'd beaten some good schools. Kids who usually ignored everything that wasn't on the sports page stopped us in the hall to congratulate us, and I was an overnight school celebrity. Marris would have freaked if he'd known about it; half of Norwell now knew Donna White. Our "low profile" was blown completely. Mom's boss even told her to pass his congratulations on.

Greg and the rest were upset with me, and I couldn't blame them. Here we were the heroes of the school, or close to it, and instead of being happy about it, I went around scowling. Well, not actually scowling. I'd learned how to act better than that, and I don't think most of the kids realized what was going on. But the rest of the *Arsenic and Old Lace* cast did, and after the first couple of days, they started getting mad.

It came to a head Wednesday night, when we had our technical rehearsal. We were scheduled to do the play for Norwell on Friday, and ticket sales had boomed since the contest. In fact, Miss Ahrens announced at the start of the rehearsal that we would go ahead and do an extra performance on Saturday night. The others cheered, since that was the best a senior play had ever done, and after a moment I joined in.

A technical rehearsal is pretty boring, mainly checking light cues and curtains, things like that, so it's not surprising that my mind started wandering again. But after I missed the fourth cue in a row, Greg called a halt.

"Earth calling Donna," he said. I smiled at him, but he wasn't trying to be amusing.

"Sorry, Greg," I said. "I guess my mind was someplace else."

"It's been someplace else all *week*," Tina complained. "The way you act, you'd think we'd lost the contest."

"Take it easy, gang." Miss Ahrens had been seated halfway to the back of the auditorium, taking notes. Now she came up to the stage and laid her clipboard down on the little table we used in the play. The Kool-Aid rocked and Tina steadied the decanter.

"Donna, you did great in the contest, but you've just been walking through the part ever since," Miss Ahrens went on. "I know that photo upset you. If any of the other students have been giving you a hard time about . . ."

"No, really, everyone's been great," I said hastily. That was funny, what she'd said about my doing so well in the contest. I hadn't really been thinking about the play at all during the contest; I'd been on automatic pilot.

"Then you're just rattled from the applause," she said firmly. "It happens. Most people get the jitters before a performance, but sometimes it works the other way. This is your first play, isn't it? Hearing applause for the first time can get to you, make you afraid that you'll never be able to act again. But it's just a different type of stage fright, and you'll do fine Friday. Now, let's go on."

She picked up the clipboard and headed

27

back to her seat. Greg came over and asked in an undertone, "Is she right?"

"I guess so," I said. I was still uncomfortable being the center of attention, but until the play was over, there was nothing I could do about it. I swore to myself that from now on I would keep a profile so low that even Inspector Marris couldn't complain.

"Well, snap out of it," he said. "We go on the day after tomorrow." He looked around and raised his voice so everyone could hear. "All right, let's take it from my entrance on page seventeen. . . ."

We went on, and this time I managed to keep my mind on what I was doing. At least I didn't blow any more cues. But it was a pretty mechanical performance. For the technical rehearsal, great acting isn't important, but it was almost our last run-through, and the others were giving it a lot more than I was.

It was past midnight when we finished. On the way out, Tina said, "Boy, I hope you wake up before Friday night, Donna, or we're going to be *dead*. What's with you? All week you've been acting like you're someone else."

She didn't know, she *couldn't* have, how right she was, but I still jumped. Greg took me home as usual, but we didn't say much on the way. He left without kissing me good night.

*　　*　　*

The next day after school, I met Mom at the shopping mall. She'd taken off work early for once. Prom was the following weekend, and she had decided we could afford the dress I'd been wanting. What she didn't say, but what I knew we were both thinking, was that it might be my last chance to have some fun as a Norwell High School senior. While I'd been at rehearsal the night before, Inspector Marris had called about the newspaper article.

He'd been furious. He said that photographs had a way of turning up in the most inconvenient places. According to Mom, he'd been ready to pull us out of Norwell right then. She had argued him out of it, for the time being at any rate. Maybe I'd get to graduate before they moved us. But I had a feeling I wasn't going to be Donna White for very much longer.

While we were in the changing room at the dress store, I came as close as I dared to the subject. "Did Inspector Marris say he was coming to Norwell soon?"

"*Hush!*" Mom whispered. She poked her head out through the curtains, then came back and started tugging at the zipper on the dress I was trying on. "I think this one's too small, Donna," she said in a normal tone. She lowered her voice and added, "No, he didn't say he was coming. But I don't think we should talk about it in public."

The dressing room wasn't exactly what I would have called public, but I shut up anyway. At least he hadn't said he was coming. They might not move us after all. But I was sick of all the sneaking around. I couldn't even talk to my own mother in a store without worrying some-one might overhear the wrong thing.

I got back into my jeans, and Mom arranged for us to pick up the dress the following week. At least Mom thought we'd be here that long. I glanced at my watch. Our final rehearsal started in another hour; I'd have to hurry up.

It was raining when we came out, and we hurried toward the car. Mom hadn't been able to find a spot close to the store, and I was afraid we'd be soaked by the time we got there. We were almost there when I heard a long blast on someone's horn. I looked over my shoulder just in time to see a car's headlights.

It was speeding straight at us.

~ Three ~

The horn was still blaring somewhere behind us. I gasped and shoved Mom sideways, between two parked cars, and stumbled after her as the car zoomed past. It missed us by no more than a few inches. I felt the rush of air on my legs as I fell on top of my mother.

"Donna, what . . ."

Mom tried to sit up, but I was still on top of her. I scrambled to my feet, banging my head against the side mirror of one of the parked cars. The car that had almost hit us hadn't bothered to stop, and as I looked around, I saw it leaving the parking lot. I hadn't recognized it, but I have trouble telling cars apart unless I recognize a bumper sticker. It was just a big black automobile with a reckless driver, as far as I was concerned. I had no idea of the make, or anything like that.

It turned onto Main Street with a squeal of tires, just as another car stopped by us. I pulled Mom to her feet.

"Donna! Are you guys all right?" It was Greg.

"Yeah, we're fine," I said. "Just wet." Actually, my head was sore where I'd bumped it, and Mom probably had some bruises from my landing on her, but for the most part we were unharmed. We were both soaked, though, since there was a puddle between the cars. It was raining harder now.

"That car tried to hit us," Mom said. Her voice was low, but Greg heard her.

"I don't think they were trying to hurt you," he said. "Some idiots think it's a big game to make people jump."

It hadn't seemed like a game to me, but Greg was right. I'd seen jerks like that myself. I'd never been a target before, though, and I didn't like it.

"It looked like you hadn't seen him, so I honked." I hadn't realized until then that Greg had been the one honking at us. "The guy's out of his mind anyway to be going that fast in a parking lot."

"I really don't think it was just an accident," Mom said.

"Why would anyone do that on purpose?" Greg asked. "You're as skittish as Donna is. Like you have a guilty conscience or something." He grinned as he said it, but the joke was too close to the truth for Mom or me to appreciate it.

"Anyway, thank you, Greg," Mom said. "Whether it was intentional or not, that car could have killed us. Donna and I had better get home and out of these wet clothes."

"I could give her a lift," he suggested.

"I'd just as soon not drive right now," Mom said, holding her right elbow. When she moved her hand, I could see it was bleeding a little where she'd scraped it.

"Ouch," I said. "I didn't know you'd hurt yourself." I dug out my car keys.

"Greg, why don't you follow us back to the apartment?" I suggested. "We can have a bite to eat, and then the two of us can go on. Have you had supper yet?"

He admitted that he hadn't, and Mom repeated the invitation. As we walked the short distance to our car, Mom said to me, "I still don't think it was just a careless driver. I may need to call the inspector."

Maybe it was because Greg had started wondering about us, or maybe my nerves during the last week were distracting the rest of the cast, but the dress rehearsal that night was a disaster. My goofs weren't even noticeable in the general mess. Greg's timing was off, and Tina kept dropping lines. Halfway through the second act, Tina blew up. She forgot her lines again, and she was so mad, she substituted some that definitely weren't in the script. The student handbook said we weren't supposed to use that sort of language on school property, but Miss Ahrens ignored it. She just had us start the scene over.

After about a million flubs, we finally finished. Miss Ahrens reminded us that according to tradition, a bad dress rehearsal means a good performance, but I don't think any of us believed her right then.

The next day at lunch, Tina was still depressed about all the lines she'd forgotten. The play was that night, and she was almost too nervous to sit still.

"But what'll I *do* if I forget my lines tonight?" It was about the fifth time she'd asked that.

"You won't," I told her. "And if you do, one of us can pick up the line for you. Or else you'll ad-lib."

"That's easy for you to say," she said. She sounded almost resentful. "You were the first one to get your lines memorized, and I don't think you've forgotten them once. Memorizing's harder for some of us."

34

"I've had lots of practice at it," I said. "Madame—" I stopped abruptly. I couldn't tell Tina about Madame Labrouste, my old French teacher at Lakewood Heights. She'd had us memorize tons of French poetry.

"Who?" she asked.

"A lady who used to live next door to us when I was little," I said. "I think she used to teach ballet or something. We all just called her Madame. Anyway, she taught me a lot of poetry, and I guess I got in the habit of memorizing stuff."

"That must come in handy for tests," Tina said.

"Yeah."

I hadn't slipped like that in weeks. Dating Greg and working on the play had made it easier for me to concentrate on my new life here in Norwell. Seeing Mr. Dillman had brought all my old memories back, the good ones along with the bad.

Mentioning a teacher's name might not seem like a big deal, but Inspector Marris had warned us about little things like that. My school records had been faked, for example, so it looked as if I'd attended Rochester High in New York, not Lakewood Heights High in Pennsylvania. All the classes and grades were right, but I'd never been near Rochester in my life. If I talked about Madame Labrouste and someone in Norwell had a cousin or something who lived in Rochester, it could cause trouble. They might mention her, and then the cousin would say there was no Madame Labrouste teaching French at that school. It sounds pretty silly, but coincidences do happen.

After school the cast met briefly onstage. Miss Ahrens gave us a little pep talk and told us everyone in Norwell was proud of us.

"And so am I," she added. "You've been a good group, and it's been great working with you. Now go out there tonight and have fun. By the way, after curtain calls we're going to take some photos onstage. I'd like all the cast to be in them." She looked right at me when she said that.

I nodded. The damage had already been done, and another photo or two wouldn't get me in any more trouble than the first one had.

"All right, makeup call at seven sharp," Miss Ahrens said. I was glad she didn't say anything else about the photos.

On the way home, though, Greg did. "You going to let Miss Ahrens take your picture?"

"Yeah," I said.

"I'd like a picture of you myself," he said quietly. He pulled up in front of our apartment and turned to me. "We've been going together for over three months, and I don't even have one snapshot. I want a picture of my girlfriend."

"Greg, don't ask me for that," I said. "Please, just don't."

"*Why*, Donna? It doesn't make any sense."

"I know," I said miserably. "But I can't do it."

"A picture of you in costume isn't the same thing," he said. "I wouldn't want to keep that in my wallet or on my night table."

I laughed, but it wasn't very funny, and I don't think he meant it as a joke.

I didn't want much supper that night—I was too nervous. Mom didn't eat much either. When I asked why, she shoved her plate back and didn't say anything for a minute. Finally she stood up and started putting the dishes in the sink.

"I'm wondering if I should skip the Cottinghams' party after the play tonight," she said.

"Huh? Why?"

"That car yesterday—I didn't call Inspector Marris, but it bothers me." She frowned as she ran water on the dishes and left them to soak. "With that picture in the paper, and what he said when he saw it, I just thought maybe I've been a little too noticeable lately."

"I've been too noticeable, you mean," I said.

"Anyway, I'm thinking about calling the Cottinghams and canceling."

She looked unhappy, and it was easy to figure out why. Moving to Norwell had been harder on Mom, in a lot of ways, than it had been on me. Back in Lakewood Heights she'd known a lot of people and been busy all the time. Here there was nothing for her to do. She spent most of her free time staring at the TV, even watching the talk shows. Mom *hated* talk shows.

I had school, and Greg, and the play. All she had was her job, and she didn't enjoy it—it was too boring. But Tina's folks were as friendly as Tina was, and they'd been over a few times. They were the only people Mom could consider friends in Norwell. After the play they were having a party for the parents of all the cast members, while we had our cast party onstage. I knew Mom had really been looking forward to a night out.

"I don't care what the program says, you can't sit home all the time," I said. "If you ask me, missing the party would be a lot more conspicuous than going to it."

"It won't be forever," she said. "If they ever start the next trial—" They were supposed to have another trial for Mr. Dillman, but it had been put off several times.

"You can't totally give up your life until then," I argued.

"I guess you're right," she said. "Maybe I will

go to the party. Right now we'd better get going."

We drove to the school in silence. Instead of thinking about the play, I was thinking about the program. I didn't want to spend the rest of my life on the run, and I didn't want Mom to, either. I was tired of lying, too. Especially to Greg. I promised myself that someday, somehow, I was going to tell him the truth.

After the lousy dress rehearsal and the rotten week, I expected the play to be a catastrophe, but it wasn't. Miss Ahrens's superstition seemed to work, and we clicked from the moment the curtain opened on the first act.

At the contest I'd been so rattled, I couldn't remember saying my lines, but for some reason I had fun that night. I'm not sure why, as I'd been miserable since returning from Chicago. But somehow I made myself forget all about Mr. Dillman and murders and the program, and concentrated on the play.

It was the best performance any of us had done, even better than the contest. Greg was funnier than ever, and Tina remembered all her lines perfectly. The audience laughed in all the right places, and at the end we got a standing ovation. The applause went on and on and on.

Since everyone's family and friends came up

as soon as the curtain calls were over, there were too many extra people onstage afterward for Miss Ahrens to take pictures. She asked us to leave our costumes on for a while longer. The cast party wouldn't start until everyone else went home, and she decided she'd take the pictures then.

I introduced Mom to Miss Ahrens. This was the first time Mom had visited the school; none of the teachers knew her.

"Miss Ahrens, this is my mother," I said. It was weird. In all the excitement, I almost forgot Mom's new name. "Mary White."

"I'm so pleased to meet you, Mrs. White," Miss Ahrens said. "Working with Donna has been a lot of fun this semester. It's a shame we didn't get to have her here at Norwell sooner."

"Donna's enjoyed being in the play," Mom said. It was true, but I noticed what Mom had done. It was my own trick of turning the conversation away from our past.

"Mom, I want you to meet Greg's folks," I interrupted. They were heading out the door, and we followed. A whole crowd of people were outside by this time. Most of the cast was there, still in costume and makeup, and what seemed like half the student body. The rain had finally stopped, and it was a beautiful night, clear and warm.

Mom was talking with the Florians when I heard Greg say, "*Hey . . .*" I turned toward him, and suddenly I was back in my worst nightmare, the one where I watched as Harry Leiberwitz was shot.

The man from the dream was there. The man with the gun. It wasn't a dream, though. And the gun wasn't pointing at Harry Leiberwitz. It was aimed straight at me and my mother. Greg had grabbed his arm, trying to knock the pistol out of his hand. Then it went off. It wasn't a loud noise, just a little sound like a cough.

Behind us there was a scream as someone collapsed. As more people started to scream, the gun flashed again. Mom fell back against me. I tried to catch her, but the next thing I knew, we were both down on the sidewalk.

My mother had been shot.

~ Four ~

"*Mom!*"

Mom was half in my lap, pinning my legs to the sidewalk. I couldn't see the man with the gun anymore. Around us people were still screaming. Just as when Harry got killed, I could hear everything, but it didn't seem to have anything to do with me. My lap was filled with a warm wetness: Mom's blood. She was dying in my lap.

"Donna?" She whispered my name, and I bent over to listen.

"I'm here, Mom. Just hang on, you're going to be all right." The words came automatically.

"Donna, call Marris. Talk to him first. Before anyone. He has to keep you safe. . . ." Her voice trailed off.

43

"I will, Mom. Just don't move."

I felt a hand on my arm. "Donna?" It was Greg's voice. I didn't look around, but I was glad he was there. I wanted to hug Mom as hard as I could, but I was afraid to move her.

"Just relax, don't worry, I'll take care of everything, Mom," I said. The words kept coming automatically; it didn't matter what I said. I just wanted to keep talking to her. "I'll be fine, please be okay, Mom, please don't die. . . ."

"I won't," she whispered, then she shuddered slightly. For one horrible moment I was sure she was dead; then she sighed, and her eyes rolled back in her head. She was unconscious.

"That's okay, Mom, you just rest," I whispered back.

"Is she . . ." Greg asked, hesitantly.

"*No!*" I whispered. "She's not dead, and she's not going to be dead. She's going to be all right. She is."

Greg knelt beside me and put his arm around my shoulder, supporting me while I kept talking to Mom. All the distant noise went on, overlaid with sirens, but I didn't pay any attention until someone else knelt beside me and reached for her.

"No," I said, and I started to push the man away, but Greg pulled my hand back.

"Donna, let him help. He's a paramedic." I

looked up then. The man had already shifted Mom from my lap and was fastening a blood-pressure cuff on her arm, while a woman knelt on the other side and pressed a pad against Mom's right side, trying to stop the bleeding. For the first time I really saw what was going on around us. There were police cars, ambulances, and flashing lights, and a babble of sound.

"Is she going to be all right?" I asked the woman. She glanced up at me, then looked back at what she was doing.

"I can't say, miss," she said. "She's alive now, and we'll try to keep her that way until we reach the hospital." Another paramedic rushed over with a stretcher. They got Mom loaded onto it and strapped down, then started to put her in the ambulance.

"That's my mom!" I shouted, struggling to get up. My right leg felt numb, as if it had gone to sleep from her weight. "Let me come with her."

"Sorry," the first man said. "The police can bring you to the hospital, but we can't let you ride with us. Let's *go!*" He banged twice on the side of the ambulance as he scrambled into the back. It was moving before he had the door shut, threading its way through the crowd, with the two-note horn clearing a path as the ambulance picked up speed.

"Greg, I've got to follow her!" I tried to get up again, and there was a flare of pain in my right leg. I sat back down hard, almost falling.

Greg stared at me for a moment, then stood up and bellowed, "Over here!" He dropped back down beside me. "Donna, I think you were hit."

Until he said that, I hadn't felt anything. Whether it was shock or seeing Mom bleeding so much, I don't know, but now I could feel a hot burning pain along my right thigh. The wetness on my leg wasn't all Mom's blood.

I didn't black out, but things got hazy for a while. The line of fire across my leg sent waves of pain all the way to my toes. Before long I was on a stretcher in the back of another ambulance, heading after Mom.

Norwell Community Hospital was as confused as the school parking lot had been. They wheeled me into the emergency room and started working on my leg. It hurt more than I could have imagined, but they gave me some shots, and the edges of things got blurry. According to the doctor, the bullet had plowed a furrow along the outside of my thigh. He said it was only a graze. It felt a lot worse than that. But I didn't pay much attention to what they were doing to me; I was trying to hear what they were doing to Mom.

46

She was in another room down the hall, and there was a lot going on there. The doctor was taping a bandage on my leg when I saw them push her out on a rolling stretcher. There was a crowd around her, but I caught a glimpse of her face. She looked horrible, a waxy white, and there was a tube down her throat. I sat up, but the doctor pushed me back down on the table.

"They're taking her into surgery," he told me. "It will be a while before we know how she's doing. You might as well wait here. I want to keep you under observation anyway."

"Can't I go with her?" I begged.

"Afraid not." He shook his head and drew a thin sheet over me. "Lie still for a while. Try to get some sleep."

I couldn't sleep, so I lay there staring at the ceiling and shaking. Quiet tears started rolling down the side of my face. It was all my fault. If I hadn't been in the play, Mom wouldn't be in the operating room, maybe dying. I knew someone else had been hurt as well; even though I'd heard only two shots, I'd seen another ambulance.

I'm not sure how long I lay there before two men came in. One was wearing a paper suit, the sort doctors wear in surgery.

"How's my mom?" I struggled up to a sitting position.

"She's still in surgery, Donna," the doctor told me. His name tag said Dr. Harkness. "I was just in there, checking. She was shot in the liver. We could still lose her. But she's holding her own so far, and the surgeon is one of the best trauma specialists in this part of the state."

She was still alive. That was all that mattered.

"Miss White, I know you're worried about your mother, and I don't blame you, but I have to ask some questions." It was the other man. I immediately knew he was a policeman, and I remembered what Mom had said. She wanted me to talk to Marris before anyone else.

"I'm Detective Johnston," he said, holding some type of ID in front of me. I didn't bother to look at it. "We've already gotten several descriptions of the shooting, but I need to find out how it looked to you. Did you recognize the gunman?"

"No," I said. The lie almost wouldn't come out, but there was no way of telling the truth without telling the whole story.

If he noticed my hesitation, he didn't say anything about it. "What was the first thing you noticed?"

"I—Greg yelled something, Greg Florian. He's my boyfriend. . . ."

"I've already spoken with Mr. Florian. Go on," Johnston prompted me.

"And I looked around, and this man had a gun and Greg had hold of his arm and there were a couple of flashes from the gun, and Mom was in my lap." I stopped, fighting a fresh wave of tears. "I don't even remember getting hit. And I didn't see what happened to the man." It struck me that Greg could have been killed as well.

"There were three shots," he said. "You were hit by the last one, but with the shock of having your mother— Did you know Mr. Peterson?"

"Who?"

"The first victim." Detective Johnston filled me in on what else had happened. The first shot had hit a man behind us in the throat. He bled to death before the ambulance got there. When Johnston told me that, I did start to cry again. That hit me hard. I felt as if I'd killed the man myself, and I'd never even met him. He was a neighbor of Greg's who'd come to see the play. Mom and I had been standing in front of him, so the bullet had gone between us.

"The first thing we have to figure out is who the gunman was aiming at," Johnston said. "Mr. Peterson's family doesn't know of anyone with a reason to kill him. Can you think of anyone who would want to kill you or your mother, Miss White?"

I couldn't say it. I couldn't lie again, but I

couldn't tell Johnston about the program, or about Mr. Dillman. My promise to Mom kept the words from coming out. I just shook my head.

They asked me a few more questions, and Dr. Harkness checked my leg. I think he wanted to put me in a regular hospital room, but I wouldn't have let him, and he probably realized that. I wasn't about to lie in bed watching TV while they were operating on Mom. Dr. Harkness had done all he could for my leg, and I didn't want to stay in the emergency room any longer. I asked if I could wait someplace else.

"There's a trauma-unit waiting room," he said. He went to get my chart. While he filled it in and signed it, he said, "You'll need to come in and have that dressing changed and the wound examined in a couple of days. Or your own doctor can do it. But for now I think you'll be more comfortable in the waiting room." He helped me get down from the examining table and steadied me once I was standing. "If your leg starts bleeding again, or if it hurts too badly, ask a nurse to notify me." He walked me to a small room with quiet lights and soft couches and promised someone would tell me as soon as there was any news about Mom. Then he left.

I sat down on the couch opposite the door, so

I could see everyone in the hall. All the lies, I thought, all the phony stories and they hadn't worked. The program hadn't protected Mom at all. I'd made a promise to her, though. As soon as I found out how she was, I'd have to get to a phone and call Marris. I'd never used the "panic number" before, but I knew it by heart.

My eyes closed, but I couldn't leave them shut. I still didn't remember being shot, but I could see the gunman's face in my mind. It wasn't vicious or ugly, just a man's face. I'm no good at describing people or guessing ages; it was an average face, except his nose was crooked. He hadn't even looked excited when he shot Harry Leiberwitz or when he shot us. His expression had been more like someone who had a job to do and wanted to do it right.

I must have left my eyes closed the next time, because I woke up when Greg said my name. Shock, the pain medication, exhaustion—I don't know which caught up with me first, but I'd fallen asleep. I straightened up, jolting my leg. The pain woke me up the rest of the way, and I looked at the clock. I hadn't been asleep more than fifteen minutes.

"Donna, is there any news?" he asked.

"They haven't told me anything," I said. "She's still in surgery." It had been four hours.

"Donna, I'm sorry. I'm so sorry." He sat down

51

beside me. There were still traces of stage makeup on his face, streaks around his hairline, and some eyeliner under his left eye. Where the makeup was gone, he looked green.

Seeing him reminded me of how I must look. They'd gotten me out of the blood-soaked costume, and now I had on a robe they'd given me. The wig was gone, I had no idea where, and most of my makeup had been smeared off. I was a mess.

Greg didn't seem to mind. He held me for a long time.

After a while I said, "I still don't know how it started. The first thing I saw was you fighting with the guy for the gun, and then it went off."

"You and your mom were talking to my folks," he said. He let go of me and leaned back. His eyes closed, as if he were seeing it all again. "I wanted to ask Tina something, so I looked around for her. There was this guy close to us. I didn't recognize him, just some stranger. The only weird thing about him was he had a jacket, a windbreaker, draped over his arm. Anyway, I looked for Tina, and just then he brought his hand around, the one with the coat, and I saw a gun under it. I mean, I couldn't believe it, but it looked real."

Greg stopped, and this time it was my turn to

put my arms around him. He looked sick. I couldn't blame him. I remembered how I felt when I saw the same man point a gun at Harry.

"I figured it was a joke, but he was aiming it, and it looked so real—anyway, I grabbed his arm just as it went off." Greg shook his head. "I thought guns were louder. Detective Johnston said it must have had a suppressor on it. I wasn't really thinking—I tried to grab the gun, but the guy threw the windbreaker at my head and pushed me down and—he still had the gun. I didn't see what happened then—I was trying to get that damned coat off my face—but he ran, and no one else tried to stop him. I don't think anyone was sure what had happened, except the people right around us. There was a car waiting for him, but no one recognized it. No back license plate, they said. Everyone was screaming by then. I got the coat off and it was all over, except Mr. Peterson was dying and your mom was bleeding all over you, and you . . ."

"I didn't feel it," I told him. "I saw you two fighting for a second, and then Mom fell on top of me."

"The cops don't even know who he was aiming at," Greg said bitterly. I felt hollow. I knew.

Or did I? If the killer had seen me that day at Dillman's, he might have been after me instead of Mom. But it didn't matter which of us he'd been aiming for. Mr. Peterson was dead, and he hadn't had anything to do with it. He'd just been standing in the wrong place.

Greg stayed with me. I saw Detective Johnston again, and more cops in uniform. At one point a man came into the waiting room and started to ask me something, but someone from the hospital showed up and chased him away. I think he was a reporter. I didn't care; I was too tired to think. I forgot all about calling Inspector Marris. I dozed off again a few times, waking up whenever someone walked by. Hospitals are lousy places to sleep. Greg slumped down on the couch, snoring.

Finally, around four thirty, Dr. Harkness came in. "Donna? They're going to be taking your mother to intensive care in a few minutes. She's out of surgery."

"Can I see her?" I asked. I stood up too quickly, and my leg hurt so badly, I almost fell. Greg yawned and sat up.

"Just for a moment. They'll be pushing her past here. Then you'll have to wait for a while before they'll let you in. You might want to go home and freshen up." He looked exhausted.

"Is she going to be all right?"

"I hope so." I started crying again. "Right now she's got about a fifty-fifty chance. If she makes it through the next forty-eight hours, then she should make it all the way. But right now—it's just too early to tell."

Fifty-fifty. For the first time in several hours, I remembered I had to call Inspector Marris. Mom was going to make it. We'd have to go back into the program and hide someplace else, but she *was* going to be all right. I swore I'd sit in my room and never go out of the house if that was what it took to keep this from happening again.

I asked Greg if he could take me home after I saw Mom so I could clean up and get dressed.

"Sure, just let me find some coffee first," he said, yawning again. "Otherwise I won't make it out of the parking lot." Dr. Harkness pointed him toward a machine down the hall, and he left, promising to wait for me by the side entrance.

A few minutes later they brought Mom out. She looked horrible. They were pushing a wheeled stand after her with all the IVs and stuff, and they had tubes sticking into her everyplace. Her eyes were closed, and her skin still looked like wax.

"Mom?" I took her hand gingerly. It was warm.

"She can't hear you," the nurse told me.

"I know, but . . ." I broke off. There were raised voices down the hall, coming our way.

"No, you *cannot* interview the family!" was the only phrase I heard clearly; then a man came around the corner. There was a nurse arguing with him, but I barely saw her.

It was the killer.

I stared at Mom, not letting my eyes meet his. All I could think of was what would happen if he pulled out a gun and started shooting right now.

"What do you think you're doing?" Dr. Harkness spoke behind me, sounding angry.

"I just want to interview the family, Doc, see if the kid knows why her mother got shot." The gunman's voice was as ordinary as his face.

"That's the most outrageous— Haven't you reporters got *any* compassion?" Dr. Harkness demanded. "Or common sense? Orderly, take Mrs. White to ICU. Come on, Miss White." He took my arm as the orderly started to move Mom's stretcher.

I glanced up, and for an instant my eyes met the killer's. It was long enough. He grinned, a nasty grin, and reached out to the IV stand. I didn't know what it would do to Mom if he pulled out those tubes, but I didn't want to find out. Before he could grab them, I screamed, "Killer! He's the killer!" and I turned and ran down the hall.

There was a crash behind me as I ran. Dr.

Harkness yelled something, and the orderly was swearing. I looked back as I reached the door of the trauma unit. The gunman was running toward me. Behind him Mom's stretcher had been knocked over. I couldn't tell how she was, but she'd be safer if he was chasing me. I turned around again and pushed through the swinging door.

Another orderly was pushing an empty bed toward the door; I nearly tripped over it as I ran through.

"Hey, watch what you're . . ." I ignored him and shoved the bed through the doors as hard as I could, then turned and ran down the hall.

There were more yells behind me now. I turned down another corridor, looking for the stairs to the ground floor and the side entrance. My feet slipped as I turned the corner, and I barely managed to keep from falling on my face. One of those little yellow Caution—Wet Floors signs was in the middle of the hall, and a janitor was mopping the floor. He shouted at me to stop.

Instead I grabbed his mop. He had one of those big buckets on wheels, and I pushed it with my foot back in the direction I'd come. The killer came around the corner just as the bucket slopped about a gallon of soapy water on the floor. I threw the mop at him, stringy end first. It caught him full in the face, and he tripped over the bucket. I turned and ran again. The stairs were at the end of the hall.

From the swearing and shouting, the killer had broken away from the janitor and was after me again. I ran down the stairs so fast, I'm not sure my feet even touched the ground.

The side entrance was at the bottom of the staircase. I went out at a dead run. Behind me, on the stairs, I could hear the killer.

Greg was parked a few feet away from the door, the motor running. I screamed, *"Greg!"* and threw myself into the front seat just as the killer came out the door behind me.

~ Five ~

"Donna, what . . ." Coffee slopped from the cup Greg was holding as I slammed the door.

"Drive, just *drive*," I said, glancing around. The killer had stopped outside the door. He had his gun out and was aiming, a nasty grin spread across his face. Greg put the car in gear, but he was moving too slowly, much too slowly.

"Would you please tell me what's going on?" Greg demanded.

There wasn't time to answer. I put my foot on top of his and pressed down hard. At the same time I shoved the steering wheel over, moving us away from the curb.

"Donna!" Greg's coffee landed between us as he grabbed the wheel. He tried to pull my foot up with his own, but just then the outside mirror on my side of the car exploded in shards. The gunman was shooting at us. I pressed my foot down harder, this time without resistance from Greg. He wrenched the wheel around, and we skidded across the parking lot.

"Is that the guy . . ."

"Yeah." I twisted around in my seat as we swerved, trying to see the gunman.

"He was at the hospital?"

"I'll explain later!"

The killer ran toward us, gun raised, when a horn blasted behind him. An ambulance had pulled into the emergency-room drive at full speed, lights flashing, and he was right in front of it. He jumped out of the way.

"Go, keep going!" I shouted. Greg didn't need the encouragement; we peeled out of the parking lot and around the corner on two wheels. Behind us I heard shouts, and I could see the gunman sprinting across the lot to a side street, where a black car waited.

"I think they're following us," I said. Greg cornered again, hard, and I fell against the door.

"They won't have much luck if they try," Greg said. He wasn't bothering to watch behind us. We sped down an alley. Greg dodged a big plastic garbage bin and turned again. We shot out a drive, across an empty street, and through the driveway of an out-of-business service station. Then we were in another alley. It was full of parked cars and garbage cans and bikes, and our speed dropped to something reasonable.

"I'm lost," I said.

"I'm not." Greg glanced in the rearview mirror and scraped us by a massive old car, up on blocks with the wheels off. "We're behind Sixth, and there's Douglas Avenue right ahead. I've lived here all my life; I know this whole town in my sleep."

"I'm glad," I said, leaning back against the head rest. "Can we get to my place this way?"

"I'm heading there," he said. "And then you're going to tell me exactly what's been going on!"

The sun was starting to rise as we pulled up behind my apartment house. The neighborhood was quiet in the dawn light. Down the block I could see the paperboy on his bike, tossing the morning paper under people's bushes. The night had been one long nightmare—my mom had almost died, and I'd been shot. But nothing had changed here since we'd left the evening before, on our way to the play.

I said so to Greg as we went inside and up the stairs. The apartment was on the second floor of an old white-frame house. It was like most of the older houses in town, and the neighborhood was a quiet one.

"Yeah, I almost expected it to be blown up or something after that ride," he said. "Weird."

"Not really," I told him as I unlocked the door. Once inside, I took a look around. "I felt that way after my father died, but Mom said just because our lives had fallen apart, it didn't mean the whole world had ended."

"I thought your folks got divorced when you were a little kid." He scowled, and the look he gave me wasn't full of trust and love. It was time for the truth. As soon as Mom could be moved, we'd vanish again into the program. I could tell Greg the whole story before we left, especially since our troubles had almost gotten him killed.

"Most of what you know about me is a lie," I began. I went into my bedroom, and he followed me. I pulled the second drawer of my dresser all the way out and carried it over to the bed. Dumping it upside down, I went back to the kitchen for a knife. I'd managed to bring a few special things with me, despite the rules. Inspector Marris had said they'd store things for us until we could keep them safely, but I wanted *something* to remind myself of who I really was. They were in a plastic bag, taped to the bottom of that drawer. I figured if anyone knew to look for it, our cover was blown anyway.

Using the tip of the knife, I pulled the bag loose. There weren't many things in it. One was

62

a snapshot, the only picture I had left of my dad. I pulled it out and handed it to Greg. The one I'd gone after that day at Dillman's had probably been thrown away months ago.

"That's my father," I told him. "He died in a plane crash three years ago. And this"—I unfolded a newspaper clipping, a picture taken during the second week of the trial—"this is me and Mom."

"Are you going to tell me what this is all about?" he asked.

"In a minute." I picked up the phone and dialed the hospital. While I was dialing, I said to Greg, "I have to find out how Mom is. I think he pulled out her IV tubes."

Greg's breath went out in a rush. I didn't have to say who "he" was. Before Greg could say anything, the hospital operator answered. I asked for Dr. Harkness. They switched my call to about half a dozen places, but finally I heard his voice on the line.

"Dr. Harkness? This is Donna White. How's my mother?"

"She's alive," he said abruptly. "We had to take her back into surgery to stop the bleeding. Having her lines pulled out like that and being dumped on the floor—her chances have dropped, but we got the new bleeding stopped. Now, what's going on? Was that the man who shot her?"

"Yes," I said. By this time the cops had probably already figured that out. "I thought I recognized him, and I wanted to get him away from her."

"He came very close to killing her," the doctor said. I could hear deep anger in his voice. I doubt anyone had ever tried to murder one of his patients in front of him before.

"Are the police there?" I asked. I intended to call Inspector Marris, but it would take a while for the marshals to get there, and the killer had already made one attempt inside the hospital.

"Yes, of course," Dr. Harkness said. "Detective Johnston is here as well, and if you'll come back to the hospital—"

"I can't," I cut him off. "I'll call you again as soon as I can, Doctor. Take care of her."

"But . . ."

"Thanks!" I dropped the phone down on the cradle. First I had to talk to Inspector Marris, as I'd promised Mom. If he said yes, I'd go talk to the detective, but I'd do what he said.

Greg started to say something, but I interrupted him. "Mom's still alive, but she's in bad shape." I started pushing buttons again, this time dialing the panic number. "Just hang on a few minutes more, Greg. I promise I'll tell you— Inspector Marris?"

"Marris here." The voice on the other end of

the phone was as reserved as ever, but I didn't care. "Authorization code?"

"Sleeping Beauty," I said. I don't know why they made us go through that stupid routine, since I'm sure he recognized my voice, and no one outside the program had the phone number. "Inspector, it's Donna White. We need help." The code phrase, the false name—even within the program, we kept up the lies.

"What's wrong?" he asked, then he changed his mind. "No, wait, just let me speak with your mother."

"I can't, she's in the hospital. She's been shot." I had to take a deep breath to keep my voice under control when I said that. "You'd better get some marshals in to guard her right away. They've already tried to kill her twice." As I spoke, I remembered the car that had almost run us down in the parking lot. Maybe that had been the first attempt.

"What? That's impossible," he said. "Are you saying it was a deliberate hit?"

"There was a guy with a gun, and someone waiting for him in a car," I told Marris. "One of the shots hit a bystander and killed him, and Mom was almost killed. And the same guy got into the hospital about an hour ago and tried again."

"Where are you now?"

"I'm at the apartment, but as soon as I get some clothes on, I'm going back to the hospital. I want to be with my mom."

"No!" There was a pause, and I heard a sort of hissing, whistling sound over the phone. I'd heard it before, when Inspector Marris was thinking about something. I don't think he knew he did it. "Look, if you're right, then security has been badly breached. Probably that damned newspaper picture. I should have pulled you right then. All right, you stay where you are. I'll get some people on your mother first—make sure she's safe. Then we'll set something up for you."

"But I want to go back to the hospital."

"I said no! We don't know who's involved. You don't want to take a chance." I didn't care about taking chances, but before I could say that, he went on. "Right now, if you go near that hospital, you'll be grabbed before you get in the door. I doubt if they'll try to kill you, but they'll probably try to kidnap you so they can control your mother."

It made sense. "What should I do, then?" I asked.

"Just sit tight. I'll get someone to you as fast as I can, and we'll go from there."

"All right," I said, and hung up.

All of a sudden I felt exhausted. And very,

very sore. I had ignored my leg, running up and down halls and stairs as if nothing were wrong with me at all. Now I know how football players manage to play an entire quarter with a broken arm. If you've really got something else on your mind, it's amazing what you can forget.

But now I remembered the wound, as it started to throb and burn. I pulled up the side of my robe and looked at the bandage. Fresh blood was soaking it. I sank down on the edge of the bed.

"Donna, we've got to get you to a doctor." I blinked. Greg stood there with a queasy expression on his face. "Sorry," he added. "I can handle anything but blood. Come on, I'll take you."

"I can't leave," I said. "Inspector Marris said I should stay here. We've got some gauze pads in the bathroom. I'll use those."

"I'll get them." He came back in a few minutes with the gauze and tape and a bottle of hydrogen peroxide. By the time we finished getting a fresh bandage on my thigh, the bleeding had stopped. The pain was worse than ever, though. I think changing the bandage woke all the nerves up.

"Think you can tell me now?" Greg asked quietly, once we had the fresh bandage on. He sat down beside me and picked up the clipping again, then read the caption aloud. "'Kathleen

Aubrey and her daughter, arriving for the Dillman trial.' Aubrey. Is your first name really Donna?"

"Yes, that much is the truth," I told him. "Mom had to change both names, but they let me keep my first one. Just about everything else I've told you was phony. To begin with, we're not from Rochester."

He smoothed his fingers over the creases in the newsprint. "This doesn't even look like you."

It had been less than six months since that photo had been printed, but he was right. I'd forgotten what a difference the new hairstyle had made. In the clipping my hair looked almost blond and the long tumble of curls didn't much resemble the short, straight style that I'd had since leaving Lakewood Heights. The change in Mom's looks had been even more dramatic. Her natural color was the same as mine, light brown with sunstreaks in the summer, and she'd always worn it in a fancy knot at the back of her head. Her head was half-turned in the photo, and you could see the knot. It had been very elegant, but since we'd moved to Norwell, she'd kept it bleached blond, done in one of those fluffy, teased styles that need a ton of spray. She hated it, but it had changed her looks, and that was what Inspector Marris had wanted.

I couldn't help it. As I looked at the clipping and the picture of my father, I started to cry, harder than I had at the hospital. Mom's chances weren't good, according to what Dr. Harkness had said, and I couldn't even be with her. And even if she lived, that plastic bag was all I had left of a life that didn't exist anymore.

Greg held me while I cried, but I could feel the tension in his arms. He wasn't happy, and I couldn't blame him. We'd been dating for three months. Discovering that everything I'd told him about my past was a lie—it had to be a shock. Finally I ran out of tears. My eyes hurt and my whole face felt puffy.

"Anyway, that's me," I said. "Donna Aubrey."

"Pleased to meet you," he said, trying to make a joke out of it. It fell flat, but I appreciated it anyway. His next words spoiled it, though. "It says the Dillman trial. Is your mom a criminal?"

"No!" I shouted. I got a grip on my temper and went on. "No, but she was working for one. She was an accountant for Dillman Brothers in Lakewood Heights, Pennsylvania. That's where we're really from. Dillman's was a waste-disposal company."

"*Waste* disposal?" He looked bewildered. I knew what he was thinking. Organized crime is supposed to be about stuff like drugs and prosti-

tution and loan-sharking, not dumping barrel-
fuls of crud. But anytime there's a way of making
fast money, crooks get into the act.

"Industrial waste, toxic chemicals, junk from
hospitals, all sorts of stuff," I said. "It costs a lot
of money to get rid of it legally, and there's not
many places that will take it anymore. Dillman's
was supposed to be doing it all legally, with all
the proper forms for dumping and everything.
I'm not sure how it was supposed to work, but
Mom said every ton of garbage had a ton of paperwork with it. Anyway, she found out that
some of the companies she was making out
checks to were phony. She got curious and
checked some of the records a little more, and
they didn't add up. They were getting huge
amounts of money from companies all over the
country, places like Illinois and Louisiana, and
she knew they weren't getting truckloads in
from those places."

"How could she tell?" he asked.

"Checks, invoices—I don't know, I'm not an
accountant. But Mom is a good one, and she
knew something was fishy. So she called the
county attorney. She spent a couple of months
copying records for a whole lot of investigators.
She didn't tell me what was going on."

I tried to tell Greg all of it, but I was so tired,
I'm not sure I made much sense. But the main

70

points got through. Mr. Dillman had been dumping stuff illegally, stuff that could kill people. They'd dumped barrels in fields, poured gunk out along roads, thrown it into lakes. Mr. Dillman would have owed millions of dollars in fines just for that. He'd also bribed people in the government to look the other way.

". . . so when the jury still couldn't decide, the judge said it was a mistrial and they'd have to do it over," I concluded. "Mom had already been talking to Inspector Marris and the Marshal Service about the program, because she's the main witness. With that much money involved, and the people Dillman was dealing with—murder doesn't mean much to them. If they kill Mom, Dillman will get off, and if he does, so will all the others."

"You keep calling it Dillman Brothers," Greg said. "Is there more than one?"

"One's enough," I said bitterly. "There used to be another one, but he died years before Mom went to work there."

"One sounds like one too many. How'd you wind up in Norwell?"

"They offered Mom some choices, but I don't know what the other ones were." I yawned and looked at the clock. It was after six thirty in the morning, and I could hear birds outside. "It's been almost forty-five minutes since I talked to

Inspector Marris. I'd better clean up and get dressed before the marshals get here." I was still in the hospital robe, which was looking pretty ratty by then.

"Will you be leaving right away?" Greg held me for a moment. "Will I get to see you again?"

"I don't know," I admitted. "It'll depend on how soon they can move Mom, but it'll be pretty soon. Maybe later—there's a way you can set up meetings through the program, at safe places with the marshals watching." It sounded pretty grim, put that way. Marris had promised to set one up with my grandparents, but he hadn't gotten around to it yet, and I doubted if he'd want to bother for a boyfriend.

I wanted a shower, but the doctor had told me not to get the bandage wet. I wound up taking a tub bath, with my leg draped over the side. It was awkward, but it felt good to get the last of the stage makeup and blood off.

I put on a loose pair of pants, so they wouldn't rub against my sore leg. It hurt so badly, I kept biting my lip to keep from whimpering. Even so, once I was dressed and had combed my damp hair, I felt almost alive.

"I think I could stand to clean up, myself," Greg said when I came out. He was right. I handed him one of my sweatshirts that was too big for me, and he went into the bathroom. I lay down on the bed for a minute.

The next thing I knew, Greg was saying my name softly. I sat up, startled.

"Sorry to wake you up, but I think your marshals are here," he said. He handed me a cup of coffee. I didn't usually drink coffee, but I needed the caffeine right then. "I just saw them pull up outside."

I took a sip and stood up. I hadn't slept long; it was just after seven thirty. Even a few minutes had helped, though. I went over to the window and looked out. Greg was right—there was a car out front.

It looked familiar.

"That's not . . ." I'd seen that same black car less than two hours earlier, when the gunman had run across the hospital parking lot toward it. And now I realized it was the same one that had come so close to hitting us a few days before. "That's not the marshals!"

I dropped my coffee cup and grabbed the phone. I heard a knock at the door downstairs.

There was no dial tone. The phone line had been cut.

~ Six ~

There was another knock downstairs, this one louder. I jiggled the phone cradle a couple of times, trying for a dial tone, but it was no use.

"No phone," I said, dropping the receiver back on the cradle.

Greg swore under his breath. We could still hear them knocking at the door downstairs. The couple who lived downstairs were retired and traveled a lot. They probably weren't home, or they would have answered the door by now. I seriously doubted that the men would go away just because no one came to the door.

"We can slow them down some, anyway," Greg said. Moving quietly, he closed my bedroom door and fastened the lock. That wouldn't delay them more than a few seconds, but I didn't say so to Greg. He knew it as well as I did.

"Maybe we can barricade it with your bed," he whispered, just as a crash from downstairs announced they'd gotten into the house. There was dead silence again for a moment; then I heard a creak. The second step on the stairs always creaked.

"We'd still be trapped," I whispered back. We couldn't fight against guns, we couldn't call for help, hiding wouldn't do any good—we had to get away from the apartment.

There was one other way out of my room besides the door to the hall. The window. I ran over to it, trying to keep my steps light, and Greg was right behind me. He saw what I had in mind and grinned.

"You ever gotten out this way before?" he asked, breathing the words against my ear. I pulled up the window as carefully as I could, hoping it wouldn't make a sound.

"Not here, I haven't," I told him. "But I did a few times back in Lakewood Heights."

I opened the window and he crouched on the ledge, judging the branches. Then he stepped down and across, onto a thick limb that angled up. Mom had asked the landlord to trim that branch before a windstorm put it through the roof. I was glad he hadn't gotten around to it yet. I followed, and Greg put out a hand to steady me.

The oak tree was solid, with thick limbs. The branch we were on was as big around as my waist, and we worked our way quickly down toward the ground. The house was still quiet behind us. I wasn't sure if the killers had gotten into the apartment yet or not, but it didn't matter. We were out.

The only problem was that we were still eight feet above the ground. Normally I would have dropped, but I was afraid to risk it with my leg in such bad shape. "I'll catch you," Greg assured me. He swung down, dangling for a moment from the branch, then dropped the remaining distance and landed in a crouch. He straightened and reached up for me.

I started to swing down when there was a crash above us. They'd broken open my bedroom door. The noise startled me, and I missed my grip and fell on top of Greg.

We both went sprawling. The pain in my leg flared, and I couldn't help yelping. Greg made some sort of noise as well, since I'd knocked the wind out of him. There was a shout from my bedroom window.

"She's out there!"

We untangled ourselves. Greg was swearing as he scrambled to his feet. He yanked me up and looked around frantically. My leg supported me; I hadn't been sure it would.

"Come on," he yelled. He still had my hand, and he pulled me toward the alley where the car was parked. After about four steps, I started moving under my own steam again. I braced for a shot, but there was silence behind us. The killers were probably on the stairs right now, coming after us. We hurried into the car, and Greg had the engine started before I had my door shut.

Once we were moving, I relaxed a little. The black car had been parked in front of the house, and we were back in the alley. As long as we stuck to the alleys, and they didn't see which way we went, we would be okay. But we couldn't hide in back streets all day. I didn't know where we should go next, but I remembered Inspector Marris's warning. If they could kidnap me, they'd have a hold over Mom. And I knew they wouldn't hesitate about killing Greg to get to me.

Greg pulled up behind a deserted garage and looked at me. "Toxic waste," he said, half under his breath. "Garbage. Those guys were ready to kill us, Donna!"

"Look, I'm sorry I got you into this," I said. "We were supposed to be safe here in Norwell—that's the whole reason for the program. Something must have gone wrong."

78

"Any idea what it could have been?"

I didn't say anything. What had gone wrong was my own stupidity.

Finally he sighed. "Sorry I asked. Well, where do we go now?"

"Marris said to stay at the apartment," I said, thinking out loud, "but I can't go back there now. He should have marshals guarding Mom, so I guess the smartest thing to do is to go to the hospital and have them call him. You'd better stick with me for a while. I don't know if those two got a good look at you or not, but until Mom and I disappear again, you might be in danger yourself. After all, you got a good look at the murderer."

"Not that good," he said. "It happened too fast. I gave the detective a description, but it sounded like about half the guys in the state."

"Yeah, but the killer doesn't know that," I said. "Please, Greg, I don't want to be worried about you, too!"

"You don't have to be," he said. He touched my cheek gently, stroking it with a fingertip. "You just concentrate on your mom. But if it'll make you feel better, I'll talk to the marshals as well." He leaned forward and kissed me lightly on the lips. Then he started the car again, and we drove on to the hospital, staying in the alleys and back streets.

Even when we got to the hospital, I thought it was better if we stayed out of sight as much as possible. Greg agreed. He managed to find a parking place around by the kitchen. We had to walk halfway around the building to get to an entrance, but at least the car wasn't where anyone driving past would spot it.

The lobby was almost deserted. The woman at the information desk was talking on the phone, and I don't think she noticed us. I hesitated. Last night I'd been taken into the emergency room as a patient, and I'd run out a side door. I didn't know my way around the hospital, but I didn't want to let anyone know I was here until I'd seen Mom and had a chance to talk to the marshals.

"I've been in here before," Greg said. "They probably have her up in the intensive-care unit." He led me across to an elevator. The woman on the phone never looked up.

A big sign on the door to the ICU told us to register at the nurses' station. Kids under twelve weren't allowed in at all. I'd never really been in a hospital before, except for the previous night, and that didn't count—I'd been too shook up to notice much. The nurses' station was just inside the door, but I could tell where Mom was without asking. A police officer was sitting in front of a room down the hall.

Greg squeezed my hand. "I'll wait outside," he whispered. "Come get me after you've talked to her." He gave me a quick hug. "I hate hospitals."

"So do I," I muttered. He went back out through the double doors, and I went over to the nurses' station. There was a bank of what looked like computer monitors, all tracing jagged green lines across grids, and a couple of nurses on duty. One continued to watch the screens, but the other smiled at me.

"Yes, may I help you?"

"I want to see Mary White," I said. As soon as I said it, I had second thoughts. If the marshals had come in, she might be registered under her real name. The nurse looked at me sharply, and her smile dissolved.

"Mrs. White is under police guard, I'm afraid. No visitors."

"I can see the guard," I said. "But I just want to talk to her for a minute. I'm her daughter."

"Who has had us all wondering where she was." I jumped. Dr. Harkness was standing right behind me.

"How is she?" I demanded. Seeing the doctor reminded me that Mom's medical problems were more important at the moment than cops and marshals and witness programs.

"Right now, doing as well as can be expected.

81

Come on, I'll let you see her, but she's not up to talking yet. I'll take responsibility, Nurse."

The cop stood up as we approached the room. The door was open, and I could see the bed from the hall.

"It's all right, Officer, she's family," Dr. Harkness told the cop. The cop said something back to him, but I have no idea what it was. I had just gotten a good look at Mom.

She looked horrible, with tubes sticking into her neck and mouth and nose and arms. Wires led from half a dozen spots on her to more computer monitors behind the bed. Some of the tubes were connected to IVs, a couple of different types. Her eyes were closed and she wasn't moving, except for the slow rise and fall of her chest with each breath. It's one thing to see all that equipment in movies, but actors don't look *sick*. Mom did.

Doctors must judge things differently, though. Harkness picked up a chart and looked at it, checked out the monitors, and said, "She's looking better than she did an hour ago. Her color's improved."

I was glad I hadn't seen it before. I was afraid to pick up her hand, with the IV tube sticking into the back of it, so I just held her fingers gently. They felt clammy, but that could have been from the temperature of the room. The whole place was freezing.

"Is she going to be okay?" I asked.

"Possibly."

"Exactly what's wrong with her?" I asked. I had to swallow before I could go on. "And—when will we know if she'll make it?" I still held on to her fingertips.

"Her chances improve every hour," he said. "The longer she holds on, the better they are. But livers are very complex." He explained: what it amounted to was that there are a lot of blood vessels in a liver, and it affects the entire body.

"And she's being monitored constantly, of course," he finished. I hadn't understood most of it, but somehow I felt better.

"And now I think it's your turn for some explanations, Donna," he said. His voice was gentle enough, but I could hear anger under the surface.

"I'd better talk to the marshals," I said. I peered around, but the cop had left. "Have they gotten here yet?"

"Marshals? Do you mean the state police?" The doctor looked puzzled. "I don't think they've been called in. Maybe they will be, to help with the investigation, but they wouldn't be here at the hospital even so. Bad enough we've got the Norwell police in here."

"Not the Illinois State police," I said, fighting to keep my voice steady. All of my worries intensified. Inspector Marris should have had someone here by now! "I mean federal marshals, United States marshals. Aren't they here yet?"

"FBI?" he asked, his confusion growing. "Donna, it wasn't a federal crime, even if someone *was* killed."

He didn't know what I was talking about. And he should have; the marshals should have been here and explained about the program. He hadn't even heard of the Marshal Service. There'd been plenty of time for the marshals to get to Norwell. Something had gone wrong.

I had to get to a phone, find out what was going on. But that wouldn't be easy. The cop was back, and behind him I saw a familiar figure. Detective Johnston.

"Miss White." It wasn't a greeting, more a recognition of the fact that I was there. The cop sat back down, and Johnston motioned me out of the room, back toward the nurses' station. Dr. Harkness followed me. "I had some men over at your apartment looking for you. When you weren't there, I wondered where you'd turn up next. I'll have to ask you to come downtown with me. I don't know what you and your mother have been up to, but it's pretty obvious you know more than you told me last night."

For the first time I realized both of them, Dr. Harkness and Johnston, were staring at me with hard, suspicious eyes. I guess it was inevitable. I mean, Norwell is a small town, and we were strangers, outsiders. And they were right; we had brought the violence with us. Even if we hadn't committed any crimes, in a way it was our fault for having come here in the first place.

I opened my mouth to tell Johnston about the program, then shut it again. I remembered what Inspector Marris had said on the phone. *We don't know who's involved. You don't want to take a chance.* Suddenly I remembered another one of the program rules: if anything goes wrong, talk to your contact before you do anything else. Don't improvise, they said. Improvising was all I'd done for the last few hours.

"I need to make a phone call," I said.

Johnston shook his head. "If you want to call an attorney, we can arrange that down at headquarters," he offered. "Your mother is under arrest as a material witness in Mr. Peterson's death, and I asked Judge Hollihan for a warrant on you earlier."

"But she didn't *do* anything!"

"I didn't say she did. But this allows us to hold you, both of you, until we get some straight answers."

I couldn't believe it, but the look on his face convinced me he meant it. Inspector Marris would be able to get us out of this, of course, but the sooner we went back into hiding, the better. And that one lone cop, now back in the folding chair next to Mom's bed, wasn't much protection. Not against these killers. I wasn't going downtown until I talked to Inspector Marris.

"Before you leave, Donna, let me take a look at that leg." Johnston didn't argue, and we headed for the set of double doors at the end of the hall. I recognized where we were then—the emergency room. The waiting room where I'd sat for hours was across the hall.

Harkness told the detective to wait there, and he took me into one of the little examination rooms. There was some blood on the bandage, and he replaced it, doing a neater job than Greg and I had done. While he was rebandaging it, Harkness told me not to move the leg any more than necessary. I didn't tell him what I'd been doing. I doubt if he would have approved of running down stairs and falling out of trees.

As he finished putting the bandage on, his pager went off. "Wait here," he told me. "I'm going to send someone in to give you a shot." He walked out, leaving me on the examination table without my pants, but with a fresh bandage. I had the pants back on before the door

86

closed all the way. Antibiotics could wait; I might not get another chance like this.

I opened the door a crack and looked out. No one was in sight, although I could hear someone talking farther down the hall. If I went past the waiting room, Johnston would spot me for sure. I slipped out of the examining room and back through the double doors, into the ICU.

I didn't dare stop at Mom's room, for fear the cop would ask me what I was doing there. As I hurried by her door, the cop stared at me for a moment. He must not have known I was supposed to be under arrest, though, because he didn't move from his chair. I figured he'd been out of earshot when Johnston was talking to me.

I kept moving, right into the waiting room. Greg was watching some talk show on the big TV, but he spotted me as soon as I came out.

"How is she?" he asked, coming over to me. "You were in there for a long time."

That answered one question: he hadn't seen Johnston. "She's still hanging on, but she's not out of danger," I told him. Mentally I added, *Neither am I.* "But I don't want to stay here, Greg." Once we were in the car, I'd explain, but right now there wasn't time. Johnston or the doctor might miss me at any moment.

Greg didn't argue, and if he noticed the way

I was hurrying as we walked back down the long corridors to the elevator, he didn't say anything about it. He did ask if I wanted him to bring the car around for me, but I said no.

"What went wrong?" he asked quietly once we were in the car. "I know something must have. Weren't the cops there?"

"The cops were there, but no marshals. Dr. Harkness hadn't even heard about them." I debated for a moment, then went on. "They've got Mom under arrest, and a warrant out for me."

Greg threw one sharp look my way, but all he said was, "So now what do we do?" *We*. I smiled at him as he started the car.

"Now I get to a phone and call Inspector Marris. If he says to turn myself in, fine, but I've got to check in with him first."

He pulled out of our spot by the kitchen, and we were almost to the main parking lot when I said, "Greg, *stop*!" He slammed on the brakes so abruptly, I would have hit the windshield if I hadn't had my seat belt on.

"Back up!" I said. Greg put the car in reverse while I stared at the front of the hospital. Mr. Dillman was standing in front of the main entrance, and he was talking to Detective Johnston.

Greg backed up, then pulled around and left

through the alley. "What was that about?" he asked, glancing in the rearview mirror. I twisted around to look, but the alley was empty behind us.

"Did you see those men?"

"Detective Johnston, yeah, and some dude I didn't recognize. Where we going?"

"We're going to the nearest phone," I said grimly. "That was Mr. Dillman."

"Talking to the cop? But—"

"Exactly. I've got to call Inspector Marris *now*."

A moment later we came to a gas station, and Greg pulled up to the pay phone. He handed me a quarter.

"It's a toll call. I'll reverse the charges," I told him as I dialed. I didn't even hear the phone ring on the other end before the inspector's voice came on.

"Hello."

"Inspector, I've seen Dillman!" I blurted.

"*What?*" There was a pause, then he took a deep breath. "Donna, where are you and what is going on?"

As quickly as I could, I told him everything that had happened since I'd called him earlier that morning, and wound up with what I'd seen a few minutes before, Dillman talking to the local cop in charge of the case.

"Damn!" He was silent for a moment after I finished. I waited. Finally he went on. "It might not mean anything, but—Donna, I want you out of that town right now. It's possible those hicks are so incompetent, they didn't understand when I called, but—look, don't go back to the hospital. Right now I don't trust anyone in Norwell. I'll have some people covering that place like paint inside a few hours, but meantime I want you out of there. I could fly in . . ."

"Fly into *Norwell?*"

"Yeah, right, the sticks. I'd have to get a charter. Donna, can you get out of town, down to St. Louis, maybe?"

"I'm not leaving town while that man is wandering around near my mother!"

"You said yourself she was guarded."

"By one lousy cop!" I took a deep breath. "What's to keep Dillman from walking right in and killing her?"

"The fact that it *is* a hospital, and there *is* a cop there. He's not sound asleep. Besides, Dillman isn't the type to do his own dirty work. I don't like him being there in Norwell, and I'll get someone there right away even if I have to call in the state police. But right now I want you *out*." Inspector Marris's voice had been rising. Now he said softly, "Donna, you aren't doing your mother any good staying there, just waiting to be grabbed. Now, can you get to St. Louis or not?"

"I think so," I told him. "My boyfriend can drive me. It'll take a couple of hours, though."

"Boyfriend?"

Oh, great; I realized I'd never told the inspector about Greg. I mumbled Greg's name and arranged a place and time to meet, then hung up.

"If you don't want to take me, just say so and I'll go by myself," I said to Greg a moment later. "Our car is probably still at school."

"I'll take you," he said. "But from what you said about that guy Dillman, I don't like his talking to Johnston. No telling what sort of lies he told the cops."

"I don't like any of it!" I didn't trust myself to say anything else; fatigue and fright were catching up with me again. If I said too much, or thought too much about what had happened, I'd cry again, and I was too mad to cry.

I went into the ladies' room and washed my face with cold water while he filled the tank with gas. The station had a little convenience store attached to it, and I bought some sandwiches and sodas to take with us. It suddenly hit me that I hadn't eaten anything since last night, before the play. And I hadn't eaten much then—I'd been too nervous. It was a wonder I hadn't passed out from hunger before now.

Greg was hungry too, and we each finished a sandwich before we hit the city limits of Norwell. I opened a can of Coke for myself and handed him another one.

He took a sip, then choked. His eyes were on the rearview mirror.

"What's wrong?"

"We should have gone the other way," he said, handing the can back to me. "I think I've seen that car before."

I looked behind us. A familiar black car was about a half mile behind us, and this time there was no place for us to hide.

~ Seven ~

"What'll we do?" I asked. It took an effort not to scream. The black car was catching up fast.

"Hang on," Greg said. He pushed the accelerator to the floor and the car shot forward, pressing me back against my seat. That's the first time I've ever been grateful for Greg's old car. It was a beat-up old blue Firebird, but despite its appearance and age, it was fast.

Apparently the black car was faster; it was still gaining on us. Both cars were doing over ninety miles per hour by that point, careening down the narrow two-lane blacktop. I held on, praying we wouldn't run into a tractor or farmer out looking at the crops.

We had over a quarter of a mile lead, and it takes a while to close a gap like that if both cars are going flat out. There wasn't much traffic, or we might have wound up in a spectacular wreck. We passed several cars going the other direction, and a couple going the same way. The second car we passed went off the road as we blasted around it. I looked back. The driver got out, and it looked as if he was yelling at us. Then the black car flashed by and almost knocked the man over.

The road forked, and Greg veered to the right. The black car stayed with us. This route led into another small town, smaller than Norwell. I didn't even know the name of it—I was lost. Our speed dropped to something that was almost legal as we went through the tiny center of town, and then we were accelerating again. Greg kept blasting the horn all the way through. With luck someone would call the state cops. At that point I didn't care about Inspector Marris's rules.

As we left town, Greg hollered, "Brace yourself!" and stood on the brakes. The road made a ninety-degree turn as the state route we were on dead-ended into another highway. We were still doing almost fifty. We skidded around the corner, and the rear end of the Firebird left the road as we fishtailed. Then Greg got the car back under control and was pressing his foot all the way to the floor again.

"I didn't know you could drive like that!" I yelled above the wind from the open windows.

"Neither did I," he said. He sounded out of breath, but he was grinning.

"Maybe they won't make the turn."

"Keep an eye on them, but I wouldn't bet on it," Greg said. "That guy is good."

I twisted around to watch. There was a cloud of dust as the black car also left the road for a moment, but if anything he'd taken the turn faster than Greg. We hit a rough, jolting patch in the pavement, and I turned back around to watch the road.

"They're catching up!" I yelled. They were still more than a tenth of a mile behind us, but inch by inch the newer car was gaining.

"Close your eyes and pray," Greg said. "I'm either going to get us both killed or get us out of this."

We were coming up on one of the level railroad crossings that crisscross the Illinois farm country. An Illinois Central freight was approaching from the left, and I could hear its whistle above the wind and the roar of our motor.

"Greg, you can't!"

"Got any other suggestions?"

His right foot was pressing all the way down on the gas pedal. I couldn't hear the warning bell, but the lights at the crossing were flashing, and the gate was already closed.

"Cover your eyes!" he yelled. The world turned into a shriek as the train blew its whistle and tried to brake. I raised my arms in front of my face and shut my eyes. A second later we crashed through the gate.

There was a crash and another screech as the train whistle blew again. But by that time it was behind us. I think I screamed, but I'm not sure. It was too noisy to hear my own voice. The ground rose slightly to cross the tracks, and we landed with a thud and a metallic groan as something under the car snapped. I hadn't even realized we were airborne. The gate had snapped off, and through the shattered glass I saw it sailing end over end, to my right.

The windshield had smashed right in front of us. It looked creased, with a big dent running all the way across. I couldn't see through that part of the glass at all. The rest wasn't much better; a spiderweb of cracks spread out from the center. The whole windshield was a crazy quilt of glass patches, and looking through it was like looking through a million soap bubbles.

Greg was standing on the brake, desperately trying to stop the car without losing control. For a moment we went straight, then there was that sickening, unstable feel you get when a car goes into a skid, and we started to fishtail. Greg wrestled with the wheel and somehow kept us from spinning out completely. By the time he recovered, we had lost most of our momentum.

At least the black car hadn't followed us through. The thugs were on the other side of the freight, and it was an awfully long train. It would take at least five minutes before the crossing was clear. Five minutes can be a long time. But the train wouldn't be there forever; we had to get out of sight before it was past.

"We're alive."

As he said that, Greg put his foot back on the gas. He had to slouch down to see through a small clear spot in the shattered windshield.

"Are you sure?" I asked. *I* wasn't. My arms were bleeding from half a dozen scratches from the flying glass, and Greg's face was all cut up. I looked back. The train was beginning to pick up speed again, but it still blocked the road.

"Yeah. We *did* it. *Whooooo-eeee!*" The last yell was at the top of his lungs, but it almost sounded soft compared to the roar of the train. My ears were still ringing.

"I guess we are," I said. "If we were dead, I wouldn't feel like I was going to throw up."

"Wait till we stop," he said. He sped up a little. The car had developed a bad shimmy, and

Greg was having trouble with the steering; there was no telling what we'd damaged, but *something* was messed up underneath. The road dropped down into a valley, and we turned down a cross-road that led along a river lined with trees. As suddenly as that, we were out of sight of the railroad tracks and the black car. We'd lost them.

Greg drove for another few minutes, then pulled off the main road, turning down a dirt track that led behind the trees. Then he stopped. I felt numb. I'd been too close to death too many times now.

"Whooo," Greg repeated. This time it wasn't a shout—it was almost a whisper. "I don't believe I did that."

"Just don't do it again," I said, trying to sound as if I were making a joke. It might have worked if my voice hadn't cracked on the last word.

He put his arms around me and kissed me, a long kiss. We were both trembling. I think his shakes were from adrenaline. Mine were from exhaustion. I was tired of running and sick of people chasing me.

After a while we got out and took a look at the damage. Greg's mood dampened as we checked out the car. Most of the windshield had held together, but a lot of small fragments had peeled off the inside layer of glass. There were slivers of glass all over everything—our clothes, the front seat, even in my hair. Greg had shut his eyes and ducked before we hit, but the scratches on his face were still pretty bad. A drop of blood had dried on his earlobe like an earring. I shook my head, trying to get glass out of my hair. We both picked up a few more cuts brushing the glass off the seat.

The windshield wasn't the worst of the damage, although it was the most obvious. Both sides of the frame around it had been dented, and when we landed, we'd blown the shocks and something in the steering. As we eased back onto the road, the car started to shake again, even at slow speeds. Greg groaned.

"It doesn't matter now if those creeps catch me or not—I'm dead. My dad is going to *kill* me when he sees this wreck."

I didn't answer. I wasn't ready to joke about killing, not after this morning's series of attempts on my own life.

We couldn't go very far with that windshield. Most of the towns in that part of the state are pretty close together, but the next town was farther away than I expected. The river road we were on wound a bit, and it would have been a pleasant drive on any other day. Right then, though, I liked that highway because it didn't get much traffic. I wouldn't have wanted to go on the interstate in Greg's car. It was too conspicuous with the windshield in a million pieces, and I'm not sure it would have been safe anyway.

Greg kept the speed down, no faster than thirty-five, and it was almost half an hour before there were enough houses to indicate we were on the edge of a town. Greg pulled off the road and stopped the car, then yawned, a yawn that went on and on. I fought against one myself. I couldn't believe how tired I was. It didn't seem possible, but it was less than twenty-four hours since Mom had been shot.

"Greg, what now?" I asked. "I still need to get to St. Louis and find Inspector Marris."

"We can't make it in this thing," he said. "I know where we are. That's the Embarras River. The bus comes through here. We could take it."

"How much would it cost?" I had some money in my pants pocket, but not very much, and I hadn't seen my purse since the night before. It was probably sitting in the police station, or maybe at the hospital's lost and found. All I had was the cash that Mom had kept at home as an emergency reserve. We'd always figured if we ever had to run for it, we'd be running together. I blinked tears away; we'd never figured I'd have to run without her.

"I don't know," Greg admitted, "but I can't

think of a better idea, can you? Unless you're willing to call the local cops."

I shook my head. "The first thing they'd do would be to call the Norwell police, and Inspector Marris said not to. There's a chance Johnston set us up."

"I know he was talking to that guy Dillman, but how?" Greg asked. "I mean, how would Dillman have even found Johnston, or vice versa?"

"I didn't want to tell you, but—remember how upset I got about that picture in the newspaper?"

"What picture—oh, that one." Greg yawned again and frowned. "That seems like it was about a year ago, and it was, what, a week? Yeah, I remember. Didn't even look like you, with the costume and makeup."

"It still looked enough like me to be recognized," I said. My stomach was knotted, partly from hunger but mostly from guilt. "I told you the Witness Security Program has tight rules. Well, most of them come down to *Don't be noticed*, which means you don't let people take pictures of you, and you *don't* do things like performing in plays and getting into the newspaper. I shouldn't have been in the play, Greg. I loved it, but I should have stayed out of it."

"That's silly," he said. "You couldn't stay

home for the rest of your life, Donna!"

"That's what I kept telling Mom. And now she's in the hospital, because I didn't want to stay home."

"Bull!" He glared at me. "You can't blame yourself because some criminal wants to kill your mother. She didn't make those guys break the law, and neither did you. It's their fault, not yours."

"But I broke the rules for the program. I did, Greg. And Mom's the one who paid. I don't think it would have been so bad, except Dillman was there."

"Was there? Where?"

"In Chicago." I told him the rest of it, the way I'd seen Dillman in the restaurant and the article in the paper and how he could have traced me from the news photo of the play cast. All he needed was the town name, and that had been printed. It was a relief to tell Greg the whole thing. Truth was a luxury I hadn't been able to afford in a long time.

"So that's why I said it was my fault Mom got shot," I explained. "If I'd kept that low profile Marris always talked about, none of this would have happened."

"Donna, you don't know that's how he traced you. Anyway, it's still not your fault. It was more bad luck than anything else."

"Luck, coincidence—who cares? The point is, once Dillman knew where to look, it wouldn't have been hard for him to find a way to get at us. And he could have bought off Johnston then."

A car went past, slowing down while the driver stared at our wrecked windshield, and Greg looked around. "I think we'd better get this pile of junk out of sight before we do anything else," he said. He started the car, and within ten minutes we left it behind an overgrown lilac hedge in an alley. Greg had a rough idea of where downtown was, and we started walking.

The "bus station" turned out to be a small café. I headed straight for the bathroom, ignoring the curious look from the waitress behind the counter, and checked myself out in the mirror. I was a mess, with scratches and tear streaks, and a black smudge of grease on my forehead. I didn't have any idea how I'd gotten grease on me. I washed up as best I could, getting the dried blood from the scratches off my arms, and dabbing with a wet paper towel at the rest of the glass dust on my blouse. I ran my fingers through my hair.

Greg took the chance to clean up as well, but his face still looked as though he'd fallen into some thornbushes. While Greg checked on the buses to St. Louis, I ordered us both hamburgers. A bus was due in twenty minutes, and luckily we had enough money between us for tickets.

I hadn't expected Greg to stay with me, not after our hell-ride from Norwell. Maybe I should have told him just to leave me, but it was hard enough not having Mom with me. I couldn't turn him away; I didn't want to be alone with my thoughts and guilt and fears.

The hamburgers were great, and we split an extra order of fries, and even after that I was still hungry. Food can substitute for sleep sometimes, and we were both short on that. We needed to keep some cash, but I thought about getting some candy bars to take with us. Before I made up my mind, the bus pulled up out front.

It was a slow route that stopped about every ten miles, winding around and hitting all the small towns along the way. By the time we reached St. Louis, we'd be a couple of hours late for my appointment with Inspector Marris, not to mention the fact that the bus station downtown was nowhere near the place I was supposed to meet him. At least we'd be in the same town. I'd never liked Inspector Marris, but he was our link to the program—our lifeline. And I needed a lifeline pretty badly.

I tried calling him from the next stop, but there was no answer. I figured he was already on his way to St. Louis. Well, I'd try calling later on. Sooner or later I'd catch up with him, and I could tell him I'd be late, and why. I got back on the bus and tried to go to sleep.

I might have dozed, but I didn't get much rest. Everything that had happened kept jumbling together in my mind, and I kept reliving all the worst parts: Mom falling against me, the windshield dissolving into a million pieces, the shriek of the train . . .

I sat up, but I could still hear the train whistle. I looked out the window. The road paralleled the tracks, and a freight was running alongside us. The engineer was holding down the whistle. I shuddered. That sound was going to haunt me for a long time. I felt Greg stir beside me and saw he was awake as well.

"I don't think I want to even look at a train for a while," I said.

I glanced at my watch. Despite the bad dreams I'd managed to doze for over an hour. It was getting close to sunset.

The bus stopped a little later at a small town. "One hour for dinner," the driver announced, then got off. The passengers shuffled off slowly, all of us stretching and yawning. It was a grubby bus station, with a snack bar and a few rows of lockers.

I tried calling the inspector again, and this

time I got through. He wanted to know where I was, since I should have been in St. Louis by then.

"I don't know where I am," I told him. "I'm coming in on a bus, and it'll be another hour or so before I get there."

"What happened to your boyfriend?" he asked sharply.

"He's still with me. We had to leave the car."

"What—"

"It's a long story," I told him. "But we'll be there as soon as we can."

"You'll be glad to know I've got marshals guarding your mother now," he said, changing the subject abruptly. "I couldn't get a good explanation for the delay. You come straight here; once we've got you *and* your mother under guard, we can start digging into what's gone wrong."

"How is she?" I asked.

"Still unconscious, but the doctor said she's holding her own."

He promised to have marshals waiting for us in St. Louis, and I hung up and joined Greg at the snack bar. We were both still hungry. The food we bought took most of what was left of our cash, but we didn't care. Before long we'd get to St. Louis, and I could get some emergency money from Marris. I'd make him pay Greg back, too.

There was still fifteen minutes before the bus would leave. Greg stood up and said, "I've got to make a call as well."

"Huh?"

"My folks," he said, and he grimaced. "I'm not sure what to tell them, but I'd better at least tell Dad where I left the car, and what sort of shape it's in."

"Oh." I felt guilty; I'd forgotten all about Greg's parents. They must have been worried. From the look on Greg's face, he was worried too, about talking to them.

He was gone almost ten minutes. When he came back, he looked like someone getting out of a dentist's office.

"What'd you tell them?" I asked.

"I didn't tell them the whole thing," he said. "Just that you were in trouble and I was helping you and we were on our way to St. Louis, but we'd be back and not to worry. That was a waste of breath—Mom had already called the cops. Detective Johnston was over at the house earlier, and from what Mom said, I think he's got her convinced you and your mom are big-time drug dealers or something. It took me a while to settle her down."

"Did you tell them about the car?"

"Yeah." He didn't look happy about it. "Just that we'd had a little accident, and what sort of shape it's in, and where it is. I think my savings account just got wiped out. Dad was pretty mad. I won't need a car for the rest of the year—I'm going to be grounded till I graduate."

He hadn't told them how the car got wrecked, and he planned to put that off as long as possible. I couldn't blame him. I didn't intend to tell Mom about racing a freight train until she was out of the hospital and completely healthy. And maybe not even then.

The passengers were getting onto the bus, and we joined them, taking a seat toward the rear. If we were lucky, we could sleep some more on the way. The driver got on and started filling something in on a clipboard. I leaned back and shut my eyes.

All of a sudden, I heard Greg say, "*Damn!*" very softly and intensely. I opened my eyes again.

"What's the matter?"

"They must have found the car." He pointed.

The bus station had big plate-glass windows on the side facing us. Inside, the killer was talking to the man who ran the snack bar. I could see the man nodding as the gunman turned and stared at our bus.

The killers had caught up with us again.

~ Eight ~

As the killer headed for the bus door, I shrank back against my seat, wondering wildly for a moment if we could hide in the bathroom or the overhead luggage rack. I didn't know if he'd try to hijack an entire bus, but it looked as if we were about to find out.

There was a sudden hiss as the bus driver shut the door. The next moment the bus lurched forward. Through the window I could see the gunman running, but he was too late; the bus was rolling out of the station.

"We're not clear yet," Greg said as I sagged against him in relief. I knew what he meant. Buses aren't exactly the most inconspicuous things on the roads. Even at night it would be easy for them to follow us.

As we went around the corner, I saw the black car. It was parked on a side street, a puff of exhaust coming from its tail pipe. I pressed my nose against the window. As we went past the street, the black car pulled out and turned in behind the bus. I couldn't see the car anymore from my seat, and there was no window in the back of the bus. But we didn't need to see them to know they were there. They probably wouldn't try to force the bus off the road; it would draw attention, and they didn't have to in order to get us. All they had to do was follow us to the next stop.

"Maybe the bus driver could radio ahead for the cops," Greg whispered to me.

"I guess we'd better ask him to," I said, feeling miserable. Inspector Marris would be angry, and I was leery of the police in general, but I was more afraid of what would happen at the next stop if we didn't radio for help. Convincing the driver to make the call might not be easy, though. Organized crime, hired killers after me, hoods tailing the bus, U.S. marshals—sure, it was the truth, but even to me it sounded wild.

"Want me to tell the driver?" Greg asked. I think he knew what was going through my mind. A couple of days before, he wouldn't have believed a story like this himself.

"Let's do it together," I said. "In a few minutes."

We rode in silence for a couple of miles. Greg had his arm around me, but it wasn't very comfortable hugging each other with the armrests in the way. Then we felt the bus slowing down.

"Don't tell me there's a bus station out here in the middle of nowhere!" Greg whispered.

I stood up, trying to see out the front window. I dropped back into my seat as we came to a full stop. I couldn't see much, but it was enough. There were flashing red lights on both sides of the road, and I could just barely hear a clanging noise that was too familiar.

"Train," I told him. The train's whistle blew as the engine went past.

Greg might have enjoyed that race to the railroad crossing, but I hadn't. The shriek of the engine's whistle brought it all back. But it also gave me an idea.

"Come on, this is our chance," I said.

"Huh?"

"Like you said this afternoon, got a better idea?" I climbed over him to the aisle, then headed for the front of the bus, almost running. The train might not be very long. We had to hurry. Greg followed me.

The driver was leaning back, relaxing while the train passed. Through the driver's window I could see the black car alongside us, with a line of traffic idling behind it. This was the break I'd hoped for.

"Excuse me," I said to the driver. Greg came up behind me. I put on my best smile for the driver, nice and friendly and innocent. The driver smiled back. He was an older man, with hair that was mostly gray.

"Could you let us off here?" I asked him. "Our aunt Mildred lives right over there across this field, and we can hike over and surprise her."

"Your tickets are to St. Louis," the driver said. He looked puzzled, and his smile was gone. I kept mine in place. I hoped it didn't look as artificial as it felt.

"We didn't plan it this way, but when the bus stopped and I saw where we were—it'll be just as easy for us to go tomorrow. And this way we won't have to pay for a room tonight in St. Louis. Please?"

"It's your ticket." He started rummaging through a folder of tickets, while I prayed it would take a long time for the train to pass. I wanted to get off the bus before the traffic started moving. "If you've got any bags, they're going on to St. Louis with me. I can't unload luggage out here in the middle of the highway."

"No problem," I said. And no luggage, but he didn't have to know that. "Aunt Mildred can take care of us."

"Yeah, but if she gets mad at us for crashing on her, sis, just remember this was all *your* idea." Greg picked up his cue as smoothly as though we'd been rehearsing for weeks.

"She won't. You know she's always saying she doesn't see enough of us." I doubt if it took over two minutes for the driver to locate the tickets, but it felt like hours. He punched them and handed the stubs to us, then opened the door. The train was still passing.

"Should be a bus coming by here tomorrow morning at seven twenty," he said. "You ought to be able to flag it down, no problem."

"Thanks!" I said, giving him another full-power smile. I wanted to dive out that open door and run, but I made myself get off slowly, with a little wave over my shoulder for the driver. Greg hopped onto the road beside me.

The door wheezed shut, and we made our way across the roadside ditch, keeping one eye behind us on the road. The train was still shaking the ground, rumbling past less than fifty feet away.

"Head for those bushes," Greg said, pointing to a clump of shadows a short way ahead. The moon wasn't up yet, so it was hard to see anything. We started toward them, hurrying. The last car of the train clattered past, and there was the noise of car engines revving behind us. The bus was about to drive on.

"Run!" Greg shouted.

My leg gave way as we reached the bushes, and I fell sprawling onto my hands and knees. Greg bent over to help me up, but I shook my head and crawled behind the first bush, then rolled over and sat up.

Back on the road the bus had started, and there was a line of head- and taillights moving in each direction. On the far side of the tracks one vehicle pulled over to the side of the road, falling behind the bus as it passed. The killers.

We were on foot, in the middle of nowhere. It was a chilly moonless night, but for now we were safe.

I stood up as the taillights of the black car and the bus disappeared into the distance. "They didn't see us," I said.

"Yeah. Now let's go find Aunt Mildred." Even in the gloom of the bushes, I could see Greg grin. "Good story."

"Good job of picking up your cue." I grinned back. "It was the first name I thought of. I think Tina mentioned having an Aunt Mildred once."

Greg hugged me, and the next thing I knew we were kissing. A gentle breeze raised goose bumps on my arms as I relaxed into the kiss—a kiss that seemed to go on forever.

I couldn't see his face in the dark, but his

voice was husky. "We'd better get moving again."

"Yeah," I whispered. We still didn't move; we just held each other.

We might have stood there for a lot longer, but my leg suddenly buckled under me. The pain was intense. I hadn't exactly been following doctor's orders about staying off my feet. I fell against Greg. He steadied me and kissed me again. Then he asked, "You think you can walk?"

"Walking's easier than standing. Let's get going." I turned back toward the road, but he took my arm.

"If your leg's up to it, I think we'd better go the other way. I don't know how far it is to the next stop, but when we're not on the bus, they'll be able to figure out where we got off. They might even ask the driver. The last place we want to be is along that road."

It made sense. We started walking, hiking away from the highway. Two fields away from the road, we came to the farmhouse I'd seen from the bus and circled around it.

"Aunt Mildred's place," Greg said. I smiled, although I didn't feel very happy; by then my leg was on fire. Some dogs started barking as we went past, and I hoped they wouldn't come after us.

I'm not sure how long we walked after passing the farm. The sound of barking dogs followed us intermittently. We came to a couple of dirt roads, but we kept going in hopes of finding a main road parallel to the one we'd left. The plowed fields made for rough walking, and I stumbled repeatedly. My leg hurt worse and worse with every step I took.

We tried to keep a straight line, but we couldn't always, since we had to circle every time we came to buildings. Greg suggested at one point that we stop at one of the farmhouses and ask for a place to stay for the night, but I refused. Even if we came up with a good story, it was too risky. The country has its share of crime, and most farmers have shotguns and dogs. A farmer might give us a place to spend the night, but there was also a good chance he'd call the police, or sic dogs on us.

At least it wasn't too cold yet. As we walked on, though, I could feel the temperature begin to drop. Luckily we could find our way across the spring fields. The soybeans weren't much higher than my ankles, and the corn not much more than that. We tried to stay between the rows, but we probably trampled on a lot of plants.

Then I tripped on something and fell flat.

Greg knelt down beside me as I sat up. I was swearing in French, some words that Madame

Labrouste hadn't taught us and that weren't in the French IV text. It was swear or cry, and if I started crying, I was afraid I wouldn't stop.

"Feel better?" Greg asked when I finally ran out of French.

"I might if I had a bath, and some aspirin, and a bed. And if I knew Mom was okay."

"Sorry, no bath or aspirin," he said, "but I can offer you a nice big bed. Acres of bed, in fact. We're both too tired to go much farther, and I'm not sure where we are anyway. If you can manage to stand up, there's something over there that might give us a little shelter. Not that it's likely to rain."

I groaned, but with his help I got up again. The "something" turned out to be a dilapidated old corncrib. It was too rickety to risk going inside, so we sat on the ground with our backs against it. Behind us I could hear rustling noises that probably meant mice, but I was too tired to care.

"She'll be okay, Donna." Greg spoke quietly, reading my mind.

"Maybe. Even if she makes it, though, we're going to have to go back into hiding. Probably back to a safe house the program has. They've got this place in Washington that's like a fort, only it's set up with apartments in it. That's where they had us at first—I hated it. And then

I'll be someone else, and have to memorize a whole new set of lies."

"Donna—"

"I'm tired of running, Greg. But we have to."

I shifted position, leaning into the curve of his arm and resting my head on his shoulder. He slid his hand down the side of my head, letting it rest on my neck.

"Your hair looked good in that photo, but I think I like it better this way."

"Which photo—oh, the clipping."

"Maybe someday you can let it grow again, and I can decide which way I like it best."

"I'll be gone then," I reminded him.

"You won't have to be in hiding forever," he said.

I didn't say anything, but he was wrong. The whole idea behind the program was to keep us hidden for the rest of our lives. Once we left Norwell, I'd probably never see Greg again. But I couldn't tell him that. Maybe I wanted to keep a shred of hope for myself.

Someplace a few miles away I could hear the sound of traffic, but close by the only sounds were the breeze and about a million insects, and our breathing. It was starting to get a little cold, and I snuggled closer to Greg. I fell asleep watching the stars.

*   *   *

118

"No!"

I screamed and struggled, but the hands wouldn't let go of me. For a confused moment I thought it was the killer, but then I heard Greg's voice saying, "Donna, wake up!"

Greg let go of me as I sat up. It was still night, and it was cold. I wished he'd put his arms around me again; I was freezing. In the distance an entire chorus of dogs had started barking, probably disturbed by my shouts.

"Are you all right?" he asked. "You were moaning, and when I tried to wake you up, you started hitting me and yelling, something about some guy named Harry."

Harry. In my dream I'd watched the gunman kill Harry Leiberwitz, then come after me. Only my mom had been there with Harry, and the killer had caught me this time. That was when Greg woke me up.

"They killed him," I said. "They killed him just like they killed Mr. Peterson, like they tried to kill Mom. Like they're going to kill me when they catch me."

"They aren't going to catch you," Greg said.

I shook my head. "They killed Harry, and I've been running ever since. One of these days they'll kill me."

"Donna, they aren't going to catch you!" Greg repeated. He grabbed my arms, and the last bits of nightmare fell away. I shuddered, then took a deep breath.

"All right, who was Harry?" Greg asked once I had calmed down a bit.

"Harry Leiberwitz. He was a reporter who heard about the Dillman Brothers investigation and came out to interview Mom. We got to know him pretty well. . . ." I went on, telling Greg about the interviews, Harry's passion for finding out the truth, everything. Then I told him why I'd gone to Dillman's yard that day, and how I'd seen the same guy who shot Mom and me kill Harry.

". . . and that's why, even if they send Dillman to prison, we'll have to stay in hiding," I finished. "Unless they catch the killers someday. I'm almost positive they saw me."

"You're sure it was the same guys?"

"Yeah," I said. "At least the one with the gun. I never got a good look at the other one." It felt good to have the last of the lies out of the way. I didn't have any more secrets.

"And you never even told Marris."

"Or Mom. I was afraid." I hesitated for a moment, then I went on. "I think you've been having fun, almost. Like the whole thing's been an adventure—like something from a movie. Even the way you got us away from the killers today, you enjoyed that. But it's not a game, and I haven't been having fun. My mom's in the hospital, and Harry's dead."

I couldn't see his face in the dark, but his voice was quiet, somber. "You're right, it was fun beating that train, but I haven't forgotten about your mom. Or Mr. Peterson. You didn't know him, but I used to shovel snow for him in the winter and cut his grass in the summer. He's dead now. I know this isn't a game."

We were quiet for a while, watching the stars and huddling together for warmth.

"You're going to have to tell Marris," Greg said finally.

"I know," I said. "As soon as we get there. And Mom, once she's okay. I'm tired of being afraid, Greg. Of being afraid, and of running."

"Your mom's going to be okay," he assured me, "and we'll find Marris. And for as long as you want me, I'll run with you."

~ Nine ~

It was daylight when I opened my eyes again. I sat up, shivering in the damp morning breeze. Greg wasn't beside me, but before I had time to get worried, he came around the end of the old corncrib.

"Good morning," he said, bending down to give me a quick kiss. I felt a little shy; I'd never spent the night with a guy before.

"What time is it?" I asked. I shivered again. It was chilly in the shadow of the flimsy structure.

"A little after six," he said. "I've been awake for only ten minutes or so myself. There's a road not too much farther on. If we'd kept going last night, we might have gotten there and been able to hitch a ride into town." He looked aggravated, but I told him it was just as well. A cornfield might not be as comfortable as a motel room, but it was a lot less likely to be found by the killers.

After a few minutes we started walking toward the road Greg had seen. I was still tired, but a night's sleep had left me in a lot better shape than I'd been. Except for my leg. It throbbed, sending jolts of pain throughout my body, but I figured that was normal. After all, the bullet had ripped through quite a lot of my thigh. Even if I'd spent the day in bed rather than running all over the place, it probably would have hurt.

The road Greg had spotted was a country blacktop that headed back toward the last stop the bus had made. There was no sense in going on to St. Louis now; I was sure Inspector Marris would have checked with the bus driver and found out about our visit to "Aunt Mildred." I just hoped he'd figure out why we'd done it. We didn't have enough money left to get home or even buy a decent breakfast, but at least we still had the bus tickets to St. Louis. We could cash them in and get enough for new ones to Norwell.

We stuck out our thumbs every time a car went past, but no one even slowed down. We looked pretty scruffy, and I guess that scared people off. Even with the night's sleep, though, I kept moving slower and slower. My leg had been through too much, and it had decided it wasn't going any farther. Finally Greg stopped.

"Maybe we'd do better if we split up," he said.

"Now?" I asked. "After what we've been through already?"

"Not really separate," he said quickly. "Just long enough to get a ride."

There was a small billboard a little way down the road, the sort that has a solid base instead of posts. Greg went over to it and ducked out of sight. I stayed by the road and stuck up my thumb again.

The next two cars sped past me, but the third one stopped. The driver leaned across the seat and opened the door. "Kind of early to be hitching, isn't it, sugar?" he asked me. His smile was more of a smirk, but I didn't have to look at it for long, because he lost the smile-smirk and got a mean look in his eyes when Greg came out from behind the sign.

I tried to hold the door open, talking fast. "Thanks a lot for the ride, mister, we really appreciate it—"

"I didn't stop for no couple," he snarled. He stepped on the gas, and I let go of the door handle before it could drag me down the road. The

125

door swung wide for a moment, then slammed shut as he picked up more speed.

"We're better off without that creep," Greg said, coming up beside me.

"No kidding," I said. "But I don't think separating was such a good idea. We're likely to get the same reaction from everyone."

"Maybe. But let's try it again anyway. It's hitch or walk, and your leg won't take walking."

There was no arguing with that, so I went back to the road while Greg got out of sight behind the billboard again. A few more cars passed by. One honked its horn several times, but it didn't stop. There wasn't as much traffic on this side road as there had been on the main highway, but it wasn't deserted, and I still had hopes we could catch a ride. The sun was climbing, and instead of feeling chilly, I was starting to feel hot. We'd been up for over an hour now, and my throat and mouth were parched.

At last a new-looking yellow car slowed down as it approached. I smiled and waved, trying to look as if it were the most normal thing in the world for me to be standing with my thumb out in the middle of nowhere on a Sunday morning.

The car halted a few feet in front of me, and I limped forward as fast as I could to the passenger's side. Another car went past as I did. I bent down to look through the side window just as the driver lowered it. The lock button popped up as I peered inside.

"Thanks a lot," I said through the window, and waved my hand behind me wildly, trying to signal Greg to come on. "I've got a friend with me. . . ."

"Get in," he said. He made no move to open the door. A radio was on the seat beside him, and there was a burst of static as he spoke.

"Like I said, I've got a friend who needs a ride, too," I said, my voice rising in volume. I straightened for a moment to look for Greg, just as a rock came flying through the air at the windshield.

"Donna, *run!*" Greg stood beside the billboard. He threw another rock at the car, overhand and hard, like a baseball. There was a tinkle as the glass formed a shattered bull's-eye around the impact.

I stepped back from the car, uncertain. The driver reached down beside his seat and came up with a gun. He started to fumble with his seat belt, but I didn't wait to see any more—I turned and sprinted for the billboard. Greg threw another rock, then vanished behind the billboard as the driver got his door open. I dived headlong behind the other end of the billboard, landing on my hands on the gravel. I pulled myself up into a crouch.

For a moment everything was quiet. I froze. The sound of a car approaching broke the silence, and I peeked around the board. The driver was out now, gun in his hand. It wasn't the man I'd seen before, so it had to be his partner, the one I'd only caught glimpses of. He was still standing beside the car, looking warily at the billboard. Then, moving quietly, he came around the front of the car toward us. Frantic, I looked around. Greg motioned me to be ready to run, and I drew in like a runner ready to sprint. Greg's hands were full of the sharp gravel that surrounded the billboard.

The driver made a sudden rush for Greg's end of the billboard, and I took off, out into the road. Behind me I heard a scuffle and shouts. Without thinking, I raised my hands like a cop directing traffic. There was a squeal of brakes as the car I'd heard, an old sedan, skidded to a stop, only a few feet away from me.

A woman about my mom's age stuck her head out the side window and yelled, "Are you *crazy?*" as Greg came out and ran toward us. I grabbed for the passenger's door and yanked it open just as he reached me.

"He's trying to kill us! Help us!" I threw myself into the front seat and Greg crowded in behind me. The driver of the yellow car came out from behind the billboard. He was rubbing at his

128

eyes with his left hand, but the gun was still in his right, and he raised it and fired.

The wild shot was more persuasive than anything Greg or I could have said. The woman behind the wheel threw the car in gear and pushed the gas pedal to the floor. Greg managed to shut the door; then we both hung on as the car tore away.

"Greg, how did you know?" I asked. We were both wedged into one bucket seat. The woman glanced at us, but she kept her foot down.

"Who was that guy?" she demanded. "That was a gunshot!"

"Yeah," Greg said. His voice was grim. "Lady, I'm sorry we got you into this, but that guy was trying to kill us." The yellow car had pulled onto the road behind us.

"Well, he can't shoot you if he can't catch you," the woman said, her voice determined. "Town's just ahead, and I'm heading right to the police station."

"The car was a rental," Greg told me. "I saw the front plate, then I recognized the guy. I got a better look at him than you did when they pulled up in front of the apartment yesterday."

"Who are you kids?" the woman asked.

"Greg Florian, and this is Donna," Greg said.

"Mildred Beal," she said. I couldn't help it, I cracked up. So did Greg. Mrs. Beal glanced in the mirror and her lips tightened.

"That car's faster than we are," she said, "but we're almost to Greenmoor." The first houses flashed past as she spoke. "What's so funny about my name?"

"I don't think I can explain it," Greg said weakly.

I didn't even try to explain. I glanced over my shoulder. The yellow car was right behind us.

"There's the police station," Mrs. Beal said. She turned into the parking lot at full speed, skidding sideways across the gravel. The yellow car slowed for a moment. Then a guy in uniform came out of the station. The driver gunned the engine and sped off, taking the next corner almost on two wheels.

Before he was out of sight, Mrs. Beal was out of the car, waving at the cop. "Tommy! Get someone after that guy, he was trying to *shoot* these kids!" The cop yelled something and poked his head back inside the station. "Tommy Nordstrum, my sister's husband," Mrs. Beal said in explanation. "Once they catch that guy, we can find out— Hey, where are you going?"

By that time I'd scrambled out of the car myself and was running again. One squad car peeled out after the yellow car, siren blaring. I hoped they caught the guy, but I wasn't going to wait at the station to see if they did. I shouted, "Greg!" without glancing around. Fewer than a dozen strides took me around the corner of a garage and into an alley.

I kept running.

I doubted if I'd have more than a minute or two before the police would be after me. Running had been instinct, but I was sure I was doing the right thing. All of my reasons for not going to the police earlier still applied. I was supposed to get in touch with my contact, Inspector Marris, and let him take over. And I'd be in a jail cell long before I could convince a small-town cop that my wild story was true. Also, it wasn't likely that the Greenmoor police were ready to handle big-city professional hit men. By the time they understood what was going on, Greg and I were likely to be dead, along with several members of the Greenmoor police force.

I'd gone only about twenty feet when I spotted a hiding place. Two buildings were close together, with a narrow gap between them less than three feet wide. Several trash barrels were clustered at the backs of the buildings, blocking the opening. I squirmed between the barrels, steadied one that I'd set rocking, and squatted out of sight. My breath was coming in ragged gasps, and I fought to control it, panting quietly.

Not thirty seconds later I heard running footsteps approach. I took a chance and peeked over the top of the barrels. It was Greg. As he passed, I whispered his name. He stopped and looked around wildly, then spotted me.

"Donna! What are you . . ."

"Quiet!"

"I ought to leave you here," he muttered, but already he was pushing his way through the barrels. He knelt beside me. More footsteps were coming toward us, more than one person this time.

"Mil, didn't they say *anything* else?" It was a man's voice, a stranger, and he sounded close enough to touch. I held on to the barrel, steadying it, and I think I held my breath as well.

"Just what I told you." I recognized Mildred Beal's voice. "But I didn't imagine that gun, Tommy. Those kids were in trouble."

"I'll put out a call on them. I doubt if they'll get very far. No last name on the girl?" The voices retreated along with their footsteps.

Once they were gone, Greg stood up and pulled me to my feet. My legs shook so hard, I almost fell. Running, then crouching down like that, had put kinks in the knots that were already there from pain. I could feel all the muscles twitching, and the place where the bullet

132

had grazed me felt like a furnace. I forced to ignore it. I couldn't rest yet.

"Why'd you run?" he asked quietly.

"Instinct," I said, leaning out into the alley for a quick look. It was deserted. As I pushed past the barrels, I realized what else had been at the back of my mind. "That wasn't just bad luck, that guy showing up when he did."

"Nobody knew where we were!" Greg protested.

"Right, but they knew where we got off the bus. I'll bet they've been looking for us all night. They must have split up and gotten that rental. We made it easy for them by trying to hitch a ride."

Greg was quiet, working through the steps I'd already gone through. It hadn't been a coincidence—it had been cold logic that put the killers back on our trail.

"You still don't want to go to the cops?" was all he said.

I shook my head. "I saw a radio in that rental car, one of those police scanners. The killers would know where we were as soon as the cops said anything, and I'm not willing to bet that we could keep the police quiet."

"The cops probably think we're a couple of lunatics," Greg muttered. "And they're right."

We made our way slowly back toward the

edge of Greenmoor, sticking to backyards and alleys. We crossed streets only when we had to. With my leg the way it was, I'd never have made it on my own. Not far from the police station, someone had left a garden hose running, soaking some new sod. The water was cold and had a metallic taste from the end of the hose—and it was absolutely delicious. We both washed our hands and faces as well as we could in the icy water. It wasn't a substitute for a bath, but it was a big help.

It probably wouldn't take twenty minutes to get from one side of Greenmoor to the other under normal circumstances, but we had to hide several times. Once when a squad car passed, and once when Greg shoved me behind a house just as a black car drove by. There were two men in it. After that we were twice as careful. It took us over an hour to reach the edge of town.

We made it out of Greenmoor alive, but I didn't know what to do next. We didn't have any money left, and with the black car on the prowl, there was no way we could go back to the bus station and cash our tickets in. We didn't dare try hitchhiking, even though the closer we stayed to Greenmoor, the bigger the chance the killers would catch up with us.

We had been cutting through backyards. Most of the houses in town had big vegetable gardens in back, and we had seen people working in several of them. Greg stopped while we were behind a rose hedge and pointed to the next garden. A woman was on her hands and knees, setting out some sort of plant. Behind her the door to her house was open.

"Wait here," he said. "I'm going to tell her my car broke down and ask if I can use the phone."

"Would it be better if I did?" I asked, sinking to the ground as the words left my lips. It felt so good to sit down. "She might be more willing to let a girl in."

"You haven't seen yourself," he answered. "That leg's worse than you said, isn't it? She'd take one look at you and want to call a doctor."

I hadn't realized I looked so terrible. Greg must have read it in my face, because he added quickly, "It's not *that* bad, but you're all pale, and with the way you're limping . . . Don't worry, I won't be long." He was gone before I thought to ask him who he intended to call.

I watched as he circled around to the street side, then came back openly to the garden. I could hear his cheerful greeting, but I was too far away to make out the words. No one would have guessed, looking at him, that he was in any kind of trouble.

I waited behind the hedge for at least twenty

minutes. In spite of all that had passed, it was still midmorning. I was thirsty again; it had been a while since our drink from that hose. What I wanted even more than water was to get to a phone myself. I had no idea where Inspector Marris was now, and I needed to call the Norwell hospital. The last I'd heard about Mom had been from Marris the night before, and I wanted to talk to the doctor myself.

After Greg had been inside the house for almost half an hour, I started to get worried. The squad car passed by again, but I ducked out of sight. Finally Greg came out of the house and started down the road. He circled around and joined me.

"Here, have some breakfast," he said, handing me a paper napkin wrapped around something. I opened it up. It was a cinnamon roll, homemade and still warm. "That's what took me so long. I told her I broke down outside of town and hiked in, and when she offered me a roll and some coffee—well, I was hungry. Anyway, she gave me an extra to take with me."

I'd eaten half of it before he'd finished speaking. Like the water earlier, it tasted great. The food gave me enough energy to stand up.

"Who'd you call?" I asked.

"Tina. You don't want to call the cops, and if I called my folks, I knew they'd call the cops right off. It had to be someone with a car, and somebody we could trust not to say anything to *anybody*."

Greg had told her not to tell anyone where she was going, and said we'd meet her on the road. We started walking again, this time along the highway. It was nerve-racking, since there weren't any hiding places. We hadn't gone more than a mile, though, when we found a patch of bushes where we could watch the road in both directions and stay out of sight. An hour or so later Greg stood up and waved to an oncoming car. It was Tina.

We were on our way back to Norwell.

~ Ten ~

"Man, I don't know what you've been up to, Donna, but the whole town's after you," Tina said once she'd turned the car around and started back toward Norwell. "Miss Ahrens called me last night and said she'd been at the hospital and your mom's doctor was looking for you, and Greg's parents called me at one o'clock this morning, asking if I'd heard from either of you"—I saw Greg wince at that—"and I had *two* sets of cops asking me questions, wanting to know—"

"Two sets?" I interrupted. "Who?"

"Yesterday morning a couple of guys from the state police came by," she said. "I'd never seen them around town before. I figured they were there because of the shooting—nothing like that's ever happened in Norwell before. And the Norwell cops have been asking everybody in town questions!"

"What'd the state cops look like?" Greg asked her. He raised his eyebrows slightly as he glanced at me. Had they really been police? The U.S. marshals wouldn't have said they were Illinois police.

"I don't know, they were just a couple of guys," Tina said, struggling to describe them. "Maybe in their thirties? One had brown hair, and I think his eyes might have been green. Or maybe blue. And his nose was a little crooked. . . ."

It wasn't much of a description, but I knew it was the killer.

". . . and they knew about the play—that's why they were asking me questions," she went on. "They wanted to know if I knew anyone who drove a blue Firebird. They said the last time anyone had seen you, you were getting into one."

Greg and I exchanged another glance. The only person who had seen me get into his car was the gunman at the hospital. "Did you tell them?" I asked her.

"Yeah," she said. She took her eyes away from the road again and looked at us both with a worried expression. "Why, shouldn't I have said anything?"

"I doubt if it makes much difference," I said. "They'd seen the car. But I don't think they were cops, Tina. I think they were the guys who shot my mother."

"And killed Mr. Peterson," Greg added grimly. "They've been chasing us for two days. If you see them again, just get away."

"I wish I'd told Detective Johnston about them," Tina said. "I figured he already knew. I mean, if they had been cops, they would have been working with the Norwell Police Department, right? Only, I guess they weren't."

"I have a hunch they were working together anyway," I said.

The car swerved as Tina turned her head toward me, startled. She whipped her head back around and straightened us out.

"Sorry," she said. "But that sounded like you think the police were helping the murderers!"

"I do," I said grimly. "Or anyway, at least one cop."

"But Ed Johnston's my brother's scout leader!" Tina protested.

"Does that mean he has a halo?" I asked her.

"No, but he wouldn't help a killer."

"Then how did Inspector Marris's message get lost?" I asked. "Marris called the Norwell police. They were supposed to guard my mom until the marshals got there. Only, Dr. Harkness didn't know anything about the marshals, or the program, or anything. They just had one guy sitting there, and he was half-asleep. That's not much of a guard. And I saw Dillman talking to Detective Johnston."

"Who's Dillman?" Tina asked. "Who's Inspector Marris? What are you talking about, Donna?"

It took the rest of the trip, almost an hour, to explain everything that had happened. I didn't hold anything back—for however long I stayed in Norwell, I was going to be honest with my friends. Tina kept interrupting with questions, but I don't think she doubted a word about Mom and me, or why we were hiding out. She'd been there when the shooting started. She still had trouble believing Johnston was mixed up in things. Although she did admit that I had good reason to be suspicious.

By the time I'd finished describing what had happened that morning, and the way Mrs. Beal had saved our lives, we were entering Norwell. Tina drove us straight to her house. It was a good idea. I didn't know if our apartment would be safe, and though Greg wanted to let his folks know he was all right, we'd be tangled in two hours of explanations if we went there first. Tina told us that her mom had called Greg's that morning, to see if there was any news. Greg's folks had been out to pick up the car by that time, and they were both pretty upset. When Tina said that, I think Greg forgot for a while about the rest of the trouble we were in. The Florians are pretty laid back as parents go, but that car was a mess.

"My mom's over at Aunt Mildred's," Tina said as she let us in. The empty house was the most beautiful thing I'd seen in ages.

"What do you want to do now, Donna?" Greg asked me. He and Tina looked at me. I was at the center of everything that had been happening. It was up to me to call the shots.

"Clean myself up and eat," I said. I made a straight line to the bathroom, shut the door, and turned on the shower.

By the time I came out, I could smell coffee and toast. I'd showered and borrowed Tina's comb. Except for my filthy clothes, I almost looked like a human being again.

"You look good," Greg said. "Of course, you always look good. It was just the surface that was messy."

I raised my scratched arms. "Blood's a little more than messy, and my thigh looks even worse."

"You have a point," he said. He rubbed his hand over his face. "I feel pretty grungy myself."

Greg went off to shower, while Tina

scrounged up some clothes for me to wear. Since she's four inches taller than I am, the jeans were way too short, stopping well above my ankles, and the waistband was too tight, but they were clean. The big sweatshirt was no problem—it fit fine. Greg came out just as I finished my first piece of toast.

"Now you look great," he said. I smiled, but my stomach was knotting with something a whole lot like the butterflies I'd felt when I auditioned for the play last February. I knew what I needed to do, and I was afraid.

"I'm going to have to get back into the hospital," I said quietly. "I can't leave town again—those guys are probably watching the roads, and I've got no idea if Inspector Marris is still in St. Louis. And I can't wait for him any longer. He's got marshals watching Mom now, so I'll have to get to them."

"What if Johnston's with them?" Greg asked.

"Then I find out if he really was mixed up in it," I said. I reached for the phone. "I'd better call first."

I dialed the number and asked for Dr. Harkness. They put me through to him right away.

"Dr. Harkness?" I began. "It's Donna White."

"You'd best get over here right away," he said abruptly. "It's a good thing you called. Your

144

mother has taken a turn for the worse, and if you want to— Well, just get here. Quickly."

He hung up and I put down the phone, feeling numb.

"Donna?"

I stood up and almost knocked the chair over. Greg put his arm around me as I took a step or two toward the door. All the fear, all the panic, it was all gone. I felt as though someone had frozen my insides.

"Donna, what is it?" Greg asked me, his arm wrapped tightly around my waist. Tina stood up as well. She looked frightened.

"Can—will you take me to the hospital, Tina?" I licked my lips, which suddenly were dryer than they'd ever been. "It's Mom. The doctor told me to come right away."

"Oh, no," Tina moaned softly. Greg said something under his breath and hugged me roughly. His touch broke the spell that had me frozen, and all at once I came back to life. My throat was so tight, I could barely breathe, and my heart was pounding in my chest. I don't remember if we said anything else, but within minutes we were all in the car, heading for the hospital. Tears were pouring down my cheeks, but I wasn't sobbing. I didn't even know they were there until Greg reached over and wiped them away.

It couldn't have taken more than five minutes to get to the hospital from Tina's house, but it felt like an eternity. In a way, it might have been better if I'd been driving; the mechanics of operating the car would have given my mind something to hold on to.

Tina pulled up in front of the main entrance and slowed the car. I was racing through the double doors even before the car had completely stopped. Behind me I heard Tina and Greg clambering to catch up. A woman came around the desk as we burst in and started to argue with Tina about where she'd left the car, but I didn't really hear most of it. I just ran for the elevator. I punched the button for the second floor and tried to control my breathing, wondering vaguely why I'd never realized before how slow elevators were.

Once the doors opened, I sprinted down the hall, slowing only when I came to the double doors of the intensive-care unit. I was afraid of what I'd find inside. Before I could push through, they opened from the inside, and Dr. Harkness came out.

"You came, then," he said.

"Is she—" I couldn't finish the question. I could barely say that much for the tightness in my throat.

"She's going to be all right," a voice behind

me said. "And you're going to answer some questions right now!" A hard hand took hold of my arm and pulled me around. Detective Johnston glared down at me.

"Let go of her, Johnston," a familiar voice said. "I told you, we'll handle any questions." Inspector Marris had come out of the ICU behind Dr. Harkness.

I'd spent two days trying to get to Inspector Marris, but right then I hardly noticed him. Turning to Dr. Harkness, I asked, "How is she?"

"She's still alive, Donna," he said. "She took a bad turn late last night, more internal bleeding, but we got it stopped and she's doing better."

"Then what—" I started, just as Greg said, "You mean that was a lie?"

After all I'd been through, it was too much. If Johnston hadn't been holding my arm, I would have collapsed to the floor. I didn't faint, but for a moment the whole hospital seemed to be rotating around me, and all I could hear was a roaring in my ears. I staggered, and Johnston steadied me.

"She's all right?" I asked. "She's going to make it?"

"That's a sleazy trick," Greg growled. He pulled me away from Johnston and held me.

"I agree, and I'm sorry, Miss White," Dr.

Harkness said. "But we didn't know where you were, and ever since you ran out of here yesterday—Detective Johnston insisted."

"Happened before I got here, Donna," Inspector Marris said. "I came by to check on your mother and found him trying to cross-examine the deputy marshal on guard."

"I'm sorry," Johnston said. He didn't look sorry. "But I'm going to find out what's been happening in this town, and my only witness—*you*, Miss White—has been running away every time I start to ask questions. Your mother's fine, and you're coming down to headquarters with me."

"Not until I see my mother!"

"She's not going with you at all," Inspector Marris added. "Johnston, you have no standing in this."

While they argued, I whispered to Greg, "Don't say anything to anyone until I have a chance to ask Marris what's going on!"

He squeezed my hand in answer and turned to the doctor. "Since you scared her half to death, I think the least you can do is let Donna see her mom."

Marris broke off his argument to nod. "I guess we can allow that. Then I'm going to get Donna out of here and stash her someplace safe while I make arrangements for transferring her mother to another hospital."

Dr. Harkness said, "I told you, she shouldn't be moved yet. I won't sign a release—" At the same time, Johnston started up again, demanding a chance to question me. I tugged at Greg's hand, and we headed in through the double doors. The three of them shut up then and followed us in.

Mom was in the same place as before, but this time there were two guards. They both wore business suits instead of uniforms, but neither of them looked sleepy, the way the cop had. I relaxed slightly at the sight of them. Finally the marshals were in charge and Mom was safe.

Marris stopped to talk to one of them, but Johnston and the doctor followed me right into the room. The last of the ice melted inside me when I saw her. She looked a lot better. They still had her hooked up to all the machines and monitors, and there were IVs sticking into her all over, but the tube down her throat was gone, and I could hear her breathing heavily. She had an oxygen clip on her nose, but I could see her face. Her color had returned, and her skin no longer looked waxy.

As I took her fingers in mine, her eyelids fluttered for a moment. The doctor said in a very low voice, "She's regained consciousness a couple of times, but don't try to make her talk. You can say a few words."

"Mom?" I cleared my throat and tried again. "Mom, it's Donna. I'm here. You're going to be all right, you're safe now."

"Donna?" At first I thought I'd imagined it, her voice was so faint. Her eyes opened and for a moment she focused on my face. "Donna. I love you. . . ."

Suddenly I *knew* she'd make it. It had been close, but the killers had missed this time. Her eyes drifted shut. She was asleep.

Everything was going to be okay.

I stood there for a while longer, holding her fingertips and hoping she'd open her eyes again. Inspector Marris and Dr. Harkness started another argument about moving Mom, while Detective Johnston watched me with suspicious eyes. I wondered if he knew I'd seen him talking to Mr. Dillman.

Greg had his arm around my waist, watching Mom's face with me. When Marris finally finished his argument, he said, "All right, Donna, time to go." Greg's grip tightened slightly; then he released me.

"I'd like to come with Donna," he told Marris.

"Out of the question." Marris shook his

head. He looked annoyed.

"Keeping kids and civilians out of it, that's one thing," Johnston said. "But keeping other law-enforcement agencies in the dark—Marris, I get some answers or I'm going to arrest you as a material witness, federal marshal or not!"

"You'll get answers as soon as we decide how much we can share," Marris said, waving off the demand. The program was federal; they didn't have to tell local authorities anything, and usually didn't. He started to hustle me out of the room.

"Wait a minute," I said. I went back to Mom and bent over her, brushing her forehead with a soft kiss. "'Bye, Mom. See you soon," I whispered. Straightening up, I said, "At least let Greg walk down with us."

Marris scowled, but he nodded. As we left, the lawmen started arguing about jurisdiction again. It gave me a chance to mutter a few words to Greg.

"I'll get word to you somehow," I said.

"What—" Greg started to speak in a normal voice, but after another look at Inspector Marris and Detective Johnston, he dropped his voice to match mine. "What do you mean?"

"I may not get to see you again for a while," I said. "I'll try to set something up. Don't talk to Johnston until Marris or I call."

"All right, but—" He shut up abruptly as the elevator door slid open.

"We'll contact you later, Johnston," Marris said.

I barely had time to give Greg a fast hug before Marris whisked me out the door. I looked back. Greg sketched a wave, and I hurried along, almost stumbling as tears filled my eyes. Despite what I'd told him, I'd probably never see Greg again.

The inspector held the door of his rental car open for me, but I don't think he was being a gentleman. As he slid behind the wheel, I asked him, "Where are we going?"

"For right now I've got a motel room on the edge of town set up as a safe house," he said. He watched the rearview mirror for a few minutes, whistling the tuneless song I'd heard on the phone before. "First of all, I have to find out exactly what's been going on. Start talking." He had pulled a miniature tape recorder out of the glove compartment, and now he flipped it on. I didn't mention the play or the news photo. That all seemed as if it had happened so long ago, and Marris knew about it anyway. I began with Friday night and the shooting. Incredible, all that had happened since Friday night. It had been the longest weekend of my life.

I was surprised he didn't take me directly to the safe house for questioning. Instead, he drove around while I told him about climbing down the tree with Greg to get away from the killers, the race with the train, sleeping in the fields outside Greenmoor.

When I finished, he sighed and flipped off the recorder, then took the next corner, heading for the edge of town.

"I'm surprised you didn't just go to the cops," he said.

"I got in trouble for not following the rules once—that was enough. Besides, after I saw Johnston taking to Dillman, I didn't know who I could trust outside the program."

"Yeah, Dillman," he said. "You say that kid knows about him? Think he'll keep his mouth shut?"

"That *kid* saved my life, and he's eighteen. Old enough to vote, even," I said bitterly. "Just because we're still in high school, that doesn't mean you can treat us like second-class citizens. No, he's not going to talk to Johnston, not till I tell him it's all right," I added, getting control of myself again.

"Just wanted to check," Marris said vaguely. "Looks like I can control the damage after all." He pulled into the driveway of a small motel, the Tour Rest. I had seen the place before and noticed the lousy pun of its name. I hadn't even been sure it was still in business. The motel was old-fashioned, the sort Mom said used to be called tourist camps, with tiny individual cottages instead of regular rooms. Inspector Marris pulled up in front of one of the units. There were no more than a dozen of them, scattered around an oval drive, each one a square building with a tiny porch and shutters and carport and a little peaked roof, like a doll's house. None of them was bigger than a single small room.

"Our car!" I said, startled. I hadn't seen it since Friday, but now it was parked in the driveway of the cottage, behind another car I didn't recognize. Another marshal's, probably.

"Picked it up at the school," Marris said. "We'll have to get rid of it."

Get rid of our car, get rid of our lives, once more make us into someone else. I followed him up the short path and stood there while he dug out his key and unlocked the door. The joy I'd felt when Mom had spoken to me was gone. All I felt now was a dull depression.

Marris stepped back to let me go in first. I took one step over the threshold and froze.

"Come in, Donna. It's been a long time."

Sitting at the table inside the motel room, smiling at me, was Mr. Dillman.

~ Eleven ~

I took a step back, but Inspector Marris stood right behind me, blocking the door. When I tried to push past him, he raised an arm to stop me.

"You know, if I didn't know better," Mr. Dillman said, "I'd say she wasn't happy to see her mom's old boss."

Instinctively I ducked under Marris's arm and tried to run. Before I could get away, he grabbed me, much harder than Johnston had in the hospital. I still didn't get it, though, not until a couple of men stepped around the corner of the unit. One of them had been driving a bright-yellow rental car that morning, and I'd seen the other one last when he'd shot at me outside the hospital the day before. He had an ugly smile on his face and a gun pointed straight at me.

"Back inside," he ordered, motioning with the gun barrel.

Inspector Marris was still in the doorway. As I took a step toward him, he turned his back on me and walked across the room, sitting down on the end of one of the double beds. Finally I understood everything that had happened. The gun wasn't pointing at him.

"Our contact," I said, looking at him. "Our safety. The man in charge of our security. *Security!*" A laugh forced its way out of my throat, past the constriction that made it almost impossible to swallow.

"Shut up!" The thug who'd been in the yellow rental that morning backhanded me. The laugh died and I choked on a yelp instead. I could taste blood. My lip had been split open by the blow.

"Sit down." The gunman motioned again, this time to the other bed. "And don't open your mouth until we tell you to, or that's just a sample of what you'll get."

I sat down and didn't say anything else, but I kept my eyes fastened on Marris. More than Dillman, more than the killers even, I hated him. He squirmed under my glare.

"I don't like this," he growled.

"You don't have to, big brother." The gunman's voice was mocking.

"If you hadn't botched the hit in the first place—"

"It was that damned punk." The gunman glared at Marris for a moment; then the mocking grin came back. "It doesn't matter. Little Paulie got into trouble again, and you helped him out like always, didn't you, big brother?" He waved the gun casually in my direction. "I can handle it now."

Big brother? I glanced at Marris, then at the killer. There was more hate than love in the look they were giving each other. I could see a resemblance between them in the shape of the chin and the set of their eyes. The gunman's—Paulie's—nose was crooked, but that could have been from a break years before.

"That's right, Petey's my brother," Paulie drawled lazily. "Made it easy, once we found out who was in charge of your mom's protection." He grinned at me on the word "protection," making it an obscene joke.

"I told you not to call me that!" Marris breathed heavily for a minute, then got up.

"What'll you tell your boss when she turns up missing?" Dillman asked. He'd been watching in silence.

"I'll just say I left her locked in here. One of

157

you can jimmy a window before you leave, make everyone think she ran off on her own again. They'll believe it—she's acted stupid enough."

The only *really* stupid thing I'd done was trust him.

"Not as stupid as all that," Dillman said. "That little piece of fluff and her punk boyfriend have made you all look like a bunch of amateurs. They've run rings around you. And you think you're pros!"

"I've got to get back to the hospital," Marris said. He stopped in front of Dillman and said, "I'll be back soon." Then he left. The other thug locked the door behind him.

Once the door was closed, Dillman looked over at me.

"You're almost more trouble than you're worth, Miss Aubrey." It was the first time I'd been called that in months. "I'm really amazed that you and your young friend managed as well as you did. But you do realize it's over now, don't you? You're going to stay here with us until we're sure your mother understands what we want her to do."

They'd never let me go, I knew that. He really acted as if he expected me to believe him. The words "little piece of fluff—punk boyfriend" echoed in my ears. Back when Mom had worked for this slime, he'd always seemed so nice, but even then he talked down to people. He thought I was fool enough to swallow what he was saying.

"What—what are you going to do to me?" I managed to put just a little quaver into my vioce, and one part pf me felt a surge of triumph as I saw the three of them relax. Another part of my mind warned me not to push it to far—not to overact.

"I told you," Dillman said. I think he meant his tone to be soothing, but it wasn't. "We're just going to keep you here until I have a chance to . . . arrange things with your mother. Talk to her. I'm afraid you won't get to see her for a while, not till after the next trial, but it can't be helped."

"I can't stay here till then!" I yelped. "That'll take months, and I have graduation and college and . . ."

"Sorry. As I said, it's a pity, but it can't be helped. If she hadn't started nosing into other people's business, none of this would have happened. Not that we're going to keep you in this dump the whole time." He gave me a smile so phony, I almost winced. "As soon as I talk to your mother—make sure we've come to an agreement—we'll take you someplace else. Think of it like being back in the program, only with us instead of the marshals." Now his smile was genuine; I think he was amused by his own twisted sense of humor.

"No." I shook my head stubbornly. "I'm not going to stay with you, and I'm not going to stay with *him*." I glared at Paulie Marris. "He tried to kill me!"

"You don't have any choice," Dillman said. "Now, shut up or you'll get hurt."

I stood up slowly, looking from Dillman to Paulie to the other goon. I was also trying to gauge the distance to the door. The other man, the one who had been in the yellow car, had locked it, but he hadn't fastened the chain. Paulie was on the bed farthest from the door, and Dillman was still seated at the single table in the room, in the corner.

"No," I said again, hysteria building in my voice. The second thug stood up and took a step toward me. "No. Don't hurt me. I don't want to stay here!" I shrieked the last words at the top of my lungs, my voice cracking on the top note.

The thug swore and came for me, ready to backhand me again to stop the hysterics.

As soon as he was close enough, I lowered my head and butted him in the pit of the stomach as hard as I could, as if I were playing tackle football. He staggered back, breath wheezing out of him, and I jumped for the door. I made it in two steps, but as I turned the latch, someone grabbed me from behind and pulled. I kicked and lashed out as hard as I could, all directions, still trying to get out of the room. I felt my feet connect with something behind me, and a man grunted just as the door came open an inch. Then something hard slammed against the back of my head, knocking me forward. The door banged shut and a hand reached past me, holding it closed.

I collapsed to the floor in pain. Above me Dillman said, "Is she out?"

By the time a toe shoved me roughly over onto my back, I had my eyes shut and let all my muscles go limp. I let my face go slack as well, with my mouth sagging open.

"She's out." That was the second thug speaking. He was still gasping a bit; I'd hit him hard.

"Let's put her out the rest of the way," Paulie snarled. "Get rid of her now, she's too much trouble."

"No," Dillman said. There was fury in his voice. "We need her until we have the mother. For insurance."

"Little bitch damned near broke my leg," Paulie said.

"You'll survive." Dillman didn't sound very sympathetic. "Now I see how she managed to give you the slip for so long. She turns into a wildcat when she panics."

"I'd like to give her something to get upset

161

about," Paulie said. "*Real* upset."

"Once we've taken care of the mother," Dillman said. "For now, dump her in the closet and lock it. Let her have hysterics in there if she wants to."

Someone bent over me and grabbed me under the armpits. I let my head loll back and tried to make every muscle in my body relax. He dragged me along, and I let my legs bang into whatever was in the way.

I was thrown forward, against a wall. I lay there for a moment, sprawled, then felt my legs being picked up and swung around, folding me almost in half. Then the entire closet shook as the door slammed shut. I was trapped.

I heard something being pushed up against the outside of the door. As quietly as I could, I squirmed around and sat up. The closet was no more than a couple feet deep, and not much longer than the width of the door itself. My heel bumped against something in the other end of the closet as I stretched my legs out. Whatever it was shifted with a rattle, and I winced at the soft sound. No one in the motel room seemed to notice the noise, though.

Not that it would have made any difference if they knew that I was actually conscious. I'd blown it. They had me, and Marris would be able to get Mom to agree to anything once he told her that. And once they got hold of her—despite my act, I wasn't stupid. Mom would walk right into the trap, and they'd kill her. And then they'd kill me. And there wasn't anything I could do about it, locked in a closet like this. Maybe "stupid" *was* the right word. I'd never really liked or trusted Marris, but just because he was supposed to be on our side, I'd never suspected him. No wonder the killers had shown up at the apartment right after I'd called him, and shown up at the bus station looking for us. I'd called in every time, just like the rules said I should do. And he'd put them back on our trail each time.

For a while I sat there in the dark, my head relentlessly pounding. Paulie had hit me hard. I tried touching the swelling, which felt about the size of a baseball, but it hurt so badly I jerked my fingers away from the wound. I'd collected a few other bruises as well, and the place on my right leg where the bullet had ripped through was throbbing.

Suddenly there was a loud rushing noise right behind me. I recognized after a moment that it was the sound of water surging through pipes. The bathroom was on the other side of the closet wall.

I flinched as someone spoke just outside the

door. "How long's he going to be, anyway?"

It was Paulie. The wood was thin enough to let every sound pass through. I smothered my gasp as my head bumped the wall in back of me.

"However long it takes him to convince that damned doctor to let him move her." Dillman's voice was more muffled, but I could still make out each word. "Don't worry, he's going to push hard. He's in as much danger as we are until we get the woman taken care of."

"The only thing big brother's got to worry about is his precious job when we grab her," Paulie said. "I sure don't like hanging around here. That punk got a good look at both of us."

"No one's going to come looking here," Dillman said.

"Still, Paulie's right," said the other thug. "Pete should have been back by now."

"I think he just pulled up outside," Dillman said. A second later there was a knock. I squirmed around as carefully as I could and pressed my ear against the rough varnished door. My heart was pounding so loudly, I was afraid I wouldn't be able to hear.

I heard the door shut and the bedsprings creak as someone sat down, then I heard Marris's voice. "Where's the girl?"

"She started acting up," Paulie said. "She's in

164

the closet with a bump on her head, and if I had my way she'd be—"

"Never mind that," Dillman said. "Well? Is it set?"

"It's set up for later tonight," Marris said. "I'll have an ambulance there at ten. I've got a hospital in Chicago waiting for her, and marshals set to—well, you don't need to know about that end, since it won't be needed," Marris finished lamely. My skin crawled when he said that. He meant that Mom would never reach Chicago.

"Any marshals riding with her, besides you?" Paulie asked.

"One. And the driver, and a couple of paramedics. And dammit, Paulie, don't kill any of them if you can help it!"

"May not have any choice, big brother." Paulie's voice was arrogant and lazy. "Not if we want to make it look like a serious hijacking. May have to crease you a little, too, just to make things look good. Otherwise, your bosses might wonder why she got herself offed with you in charge." It sounded as if Paulie was enjoying himself.

"I figured that out," Marris said. "We'll blame the kid."

"Her?" That was the other thug, the quiet one. Quiet but just as vicious.

"The boy." I caught my breath. "It might be

165

safer to get him out of the way as well. Did you know they both saw you?"

"*What?*" There was an edge of panic in Dillman's voice.

"The girl told me," Marris said. "They saw you yesterday at the hospital. I told you, you should have stayed out of it."

"Saw me *where*, doing what?" Dillman barked. "And who knows about it?"

"You lucked out, Dillman." Marris sighed. "We all did. The girl saw you talking to Johnston, which was a damned stupid thing to do if you ask me. . . ."

"I had to find out what had happened," Dillman said, interrupting him. "These hick cops wouldn't know who I was. That one never batted an eye when I told him I was a friend of the family."

"Anyway, that was why the girl thought the cop was the one tipping Paulie off. It's part of why she kept running. And she told the kid not to talk until after she tells him it's okay. So nobody else knows."

"Yet," Dillman insisted. "If he tells Johnston I was in town, they'll find some way to nail me even without the Aubrey woman's testimony!" Greg wasn't the only one who knew. We'd told Tina as well. I hoped they didn't know about Tina. I didn't want everyone I cared about to be in danger.

"He was with her on the whole run," Marris said. "No telling what she told him. He might be able to blow all of us away if he starts talking. But if we get him here and you take care of him with—with the girl—we can make it seem like they ran for it together."

"Only they didn't make it," the second thug finished. "And that leaves you in the clear as well. Sounds good."

"It even saves your stupid program's rep." Paulie laughed. "Didn't you keep saying, no one's ever been hurt on the program if they followed the rules? Blame it all on the girl, and they can still say that!"

I couldn't help it. My breath hissed between my teeth when I heard that. He was right; that was what they *would* say. Marris might not even get a black mark on his record. And Mom and I, and Greg—we'd be blamed for our own deaths. At least Tina knew what was going on. Maybe if she told Johnston, they wouldn't get away with it. But it would be too late to help us.

"Should I phone the kid?" Marris asked.

"No," Dillman said, after several very long seconds during which I held my breath. "We'll wait till it's closer to the time. Less to go wrong. And I think we'll make the girl call him. He's more likely to come if she asks him."

"If she's still alive," the second thug said.

"She's awfully quiet in there. Want me to check her?"

Before he could open the door, I thumped my feet against the wall and moaned a little.

"Leave her," Dillman said. "She can't cause any trouble in there."

"Petey, while we're waiting, why don't you go get us something to eat?" Paulie suggested.

"I told you, don't call me that!"

"Stop it," Dillman said. "You can settle your fights later. But that's not a bad idea." He started telling Marris what he wanted to eat, as calmly as he had ordered our murders. As if he ordered murders every day.

After a while my eyes adjusted to the darkness in the closet. It wasn't completely black; a thin line of light showed along the base of the door. Gradually I became aware of another source of light in the closet. I couldn't tell at first where it was coming from, but it didn't seem to be reflected from the crack under the door. I managed to stand up without too much additional noise, moaning to make it sound as if I were still half-unconscious.

I ran my fingers along the walls, searching for a crack. Then I glanced up. There was a hair-thin line of light about a foot long above my head. At one end it bent, forming an L that went on for a couple more inches. I stared at it for a moment, not comprehending; then it hit me.

It was a trapdoor. Or at least it was an opening in the ceiling. Standing on tiptoe and hanging on to the clothes rod for balance, I stretched my arm up as far as I could, but it was no use. The ceiling was several inches above my fingertips.

As soon as I'd started looking for the source of the light, I'd stopped paying attention to the murmur of voices from the main room, but they were still in there. Marris had gotten back with the food, and the smell of french fries wafted into the closet, making me aware of how hungry I was. Someone had turned on the television, and from the sound of it they had a baseball game on.

I bent over and tried to find whatever it was that I'd kicked when they first threw me in the closet. After a few unsuccessful gropes, my fingers touched something cold and slick. I realized what it was: a metal luggage rack, the sort motel rooms have for people's suitcases. Maybe it would support me long enough to reach that trapdoor. If it *was* a trapdoor.

I started to climb on it, then stopped. If it was a trapdoor, then I might be able to get up inside that peaked roof, maybe find a way out.

I'd been making small noises, moaning, trying to sound as though I were still out of it. But what would happen if I stopped making any noise? They might check on me too soon.

I dropped back down on the floor, making as much noise as possible. I kicked the door a couple times, moaned, then moaned louder, then finally yelled. I could hear someone walking toward the closet, so I took a deep breath and screamed.

Someone pounded on the door. "Shut up in there!" It was Paulie. I screamed again, wishing I could break his eardrums. "Shut up!" he ordered, pounding on the door.

"Donna!" This time it was Dillman's voice. I choked off a scream and said, "Mr. Dillman?"

"Yes, Donna, it's me," he said. His voice was smooth, without the obvious ferociousness of Paulie. I think he was trying to make himself sound like Mr. Nice Guy.

"Please, Mr. Dillman, let me out," I pleaded. "I'll be quiet, I promise."

"No, Donna, I told you before you're going to have to stay with us for a long time. And you hurt Sid." For a moment I couldn't figure out what he was talking about; then I realized Sid must be the other thug. "So now you're going to have to stay locked in the closet until you've learned your lesson."

170

"But—" I managed to put a sob into my voice. "But I'm hungry. And my head hurts."

"We'll let you eat later," he said. "Now, will you keep quiet, or do we have to leave you in there all night?"

"I'll—I'll be quiet," I said.

Paulie laughed as he moved away from the closet. Then the comments on the ball game resumed. I looked up. The line of light, what I hoped was a trapdoor, was waiting for me. And I'd bought myself some time.

~ *Twelve* ~

I waited in the dark a few more minutes, letting their attention return to the ball game on TV. Then I carefully moved the luggage rack over to the center of the closet.

I needed to wedge the wheels of the rack so it wouldn't roll once I started climbing on it. I could have taken off one of my shoes, but that would handicap me later. I tried turning it so the ends were braced against the walls, but it wouldn't stay in that position without something to hold it. Finally I unfastened my pants and slipped them down, far enough so I could reach the bandage on my thigh. I pulled one long piece of tape off. It wasn't much, but it would have to do.

I zipped my pants and knelt awkwardly

alongside the rack. The adhesive tape wrapped tightly around one wheel would keep it from turning. I hoped that would be enough.

Taking a deep breath, I reached up for the rod. I silently prayed that the rod was strong enough as I lifted my feet off the floor. For a moment I just hung there. The rod held. Then, cautiously, I braced one foot against the back wall and swung the other over onto the top of the rack. It shifted slightly, bumping against the back of the closet. Before it could shift again, I got my other foot onto the rack. Still holding the rod, I shifted my weight gradually until I was crouched on top of the rack. Then I turned loose of the rod, one hand at a time. The luggage rack wobbled but stayed in place.

Squatting there for a couple of minutes, I let my arm muscles relax. In the motel room the TV was making a lot of racket, some sportscaster shouting himself hoarse over the game. I flexed my hands, then reached above me. Grabbing the rod again, I used it to steady myself as I stood up. Once I was most of the way up, I let go. Now the ceiling was only an inch above my head. I found the line of light with my fingertips, feeling along the crack.

My fingers traced out a square about eighteen inches on a side. I pushed lightly in the center and was rewarded with a wooden squeak, a shower of dust, and an additional flood of light as the rest of the trapdoor outlined itself. I stopped again, to let the dust I'd dislodged settle and to give my heart time to stop pounding. It seemed as if my pulse were so loud, they should hear it over the television.

Dust had gotten into my eyes and I blinked repeatedly, trying to get them to stop watering. I'd been in the dark so long, the dim light hit me like full sunlight. Once I could focus again, I continued my escape.

Even moving carefully, I needed only a couple of minutes to get the trapdoor open. It lifted straight up, and I eased it over to the side. I grabbed the edges of the opening and pulled myself through, coming out in the highest part of the miniattic above the ceiling. As I eased the trapdoor back in place, I looked around, blinking against the blinding light.

At one end of the building, where the roof was only about two feet high, daylight was streaming in through a set of metal louvers. The light wouldn't last much longer; I could tell from the glare that the sun was close to setting.

There was dust all over, and scraps of pink fiberglass insulation, but there were also boards, forming a rough floor around the trapdoor and leading over to the louvers. I moved as quietly as I could over to the side of the attic. I had to

175

go the last part of the way wiggling on my belly, which sent spasms through my injured leg. Squinting against the sunlight, I squirmed toward the narrow louvers. The roof of the carport was just outside.

I pushed against the frame of the louvered grate, but it didn't budge. Bracing myself with a foot against one beam, I tried again, with no more success. I wasn't about to give up, though. I could see freedom right in front of me. Shifting around into a more comfortable position, I ran my fingers over the edge of the frame. There was nothing holding the louvers from the inside, but I noticed a small metal prong on the outside. It looked like one end of a wing nut. If the grate was held in place with wing nuts on the outside, I might be able to loosen them from inside the attic.

It took me several long minutes, but finally I felt the first nut slip. By the time I had the second one loose, the sun had finished setting. I laid the grate down on the roof of the carport, careful not to let it drop, then slithered out through the opening.

There were tears on my face by the time I managed to straighten up, from pain and from gritting my teeth to keep from crying out. All of my muscles had turned to solid cramps, and I could feel each separate bruise. But I was out.

As soon as I could move without collapsing, I crept across the roof to the back edge. I looked down. It wasn't too long a drop to the ground, and I doubted if I could do any more damage to my leg than I'd already done. I swung my legs over the side, letting myself slip slowly over the edge until I was hanging by my hands, only a foot above the ground. Then I dropped.

I dropped all the way to my hands and knees. Our car was still out front, but I decided it was safer to leave it be. Instead, I planned to head toward town, cutting through yards. As soon as I found a house with a light on, I'd go in and call Detective Johnston. Just a little while longer, and I'd be safe. As soon as I could stand again.

It was almost completely dark by now, which would help me hide. My entire body ached, but the pain shooting through my leg was almost unbearable. I was struggling back to my feet when I froze.

Something cold touched the back of my neck, and a hateful voice said, "Leaving so soon?"

It was Paulie.

Moving very slowly, I turned around. Paulie's gun was only a couple inches from my nose, almost too close to focus on. It looked huge. Then he laughed.

177

"All right, get up. Slowly. Now let's go back inside." As I walked, he poked the gun into my ribs.

It must have taken me half an hour to get from the closet to where Paulie caught me behind the carport. It took less than a minute to walk back around and in through the front door. The others were all there. Dillman looked impatient, but I could swear that Marris almost looked sorry for a moment.

"Very amusing, Donna." Dillman pointed to the other chair by the table, and Paulie shoved me toward it. I sat down. "Paulie insisted we see how far you could get. You really did quite well." Suddenly he leaned across the table and slapped me across the face. A trickle of blood rolled down my chin from the reopened split in my lip.

"I'm getting tired of your little games," he said, leaning back in his chair again. "Try anything else, and you'll regret it, I promise you."

I tried not to shudder, but Dillman must have seen me react, because he smiled, satisfied.

"You heard me." It was all I could think of to say. My mind and body numbed as despair washed over me. All the caution I'd used hadn't been enough.

"No, I'll give you credit for that," Dillman said, shaking his head. "We never heard a sound. But we went to get you out, and when we found the closet empty, it didn't take much to figure out where you'd gone."

Dillman glanced at his watch. "I shouldn't have let Paulie wait for you. It's getting late. You're going to make a phone call for us, Donna. That boy who's been helping you— what's his name, Greg? You're going to call Greg for us, Donna, and have him come over here."

All at once I remembered what I'd heard earlier from inside the closet. They thought Greg was a threat to them, and they planned to kill him as well as Mom and me. I fought to shake off the terror that was paralyzing my mind. It might be hopeless, but I wasn't going to give up until I was dead.

"Tell him your friend wants to see him," Dillman ordered. "Or that you've found out how the cop set you up, or whatever you want." He shoved the phone across the table to me. "Just make sure he comes over here, right away. And don't forget, we'll be listening to every word."

"No! I'm not going to—" I shut up, as I felt the same cold hard touch of Paulie's gun behind my ear.

"Call him."

My hands were shaking so badly, I botched dialing the number and had to start over. As the phone rang on the other end, my whole body tingled, as though I were freezing solid. *Don't an-*

179

swer, I thought, *don't be home. . . .* But Greg picked it up on the third ring.

"Hello?"

"Greg? Hi, it's Donna." Sid reached over and pulled the receiver slightly away from my ear so they could listen to both ends of the conversation.

"Donna! I didn't think—where are you?" He sounded surprised. After what I'd told him about the program, I'm sure he thought he wouldn't hear from me again for quite a long time.

"At a motel, still here in Norwell. The Tour Rest—you know it? On the road to Champaign." I was babbling. I stared down at the tabletop as I spoke, trying to block out Dillman and Paulie's gun.

"Donna? Donna, are you all right? You sound like you're crying."

"It's been kind of a rough day," I said. That had to be the biggest understatement in history. "Greg, I need some help. . . ." I went through the rest of the story Dillman had fed me, frantically trying to think of something I could say to warn Greg.

"Yeah, I can come over," Greg said. Dillman smiled as he heard that. "But I thought that watchdog of yours, that Marris, would be there. Jeez, I see what you meant about that guy."

That was my chance. "Told you he looked

just like Jonathan Brewster, didn't I?" I asked, keeping my voice light and praying he'd understand. "And he's like Jonathan in other ways, too. That's why I want to take care of this business with Johnston myself." I held my breath, waiting for his response.

"Yeah, just like Jonathan," Greg said slowly. "Look, I'll be there as soon as I can. What with the car, it might take a while to scrounge a ride."

"As soon as you can," I said, and that time I meant it. We hung up.

"What was that about cars?" Dillman demanded.

"His got kind of messed up when we were—"

"When they were leading us all over the damned state," Sid cut in. "They should already be dead, the way that idiot drives." He started to tell Dillman about the race to the train crossing, while I tried hard to keep my face blank.

Without knowing *Arsenic and Old Lace*, they wouldn't know who Jonathan Brewster was. In the play he's the killer who comes back, and he's had plastic surgery so he doesn't look like himself. That was the message I'd tried to pass along to Greg—that Marris was a killer and not who he was supposed to be. Greg had caught the name. Now all I could do was wait, to see if he'd understood the rest.

*   *   *

181

While I waited for Greg, every second felt as if it were ten minutes long. My head was pounding again, with all the bruises adding their edge of pain, and I had a new source of discomfort: I itched. Some of the fiberglass insulation had gotten on me up in the attic. But above all, I was scared. All pretense of keeping me alive had vanished with my escape attempt. This was the last chance, for all three of us.

It felt as if we'd sat there for over an hour when Marris looked at his watch and swore. "It's been twenty minutes! Dillman, I can't wait any longer. If I'm going to set things up, I've got to get started now."

Dillman looked at his own watch. "You're right. But the punk said he was coming, and we can't let him get away. Paulie, you stay here with the girl. When the kid gets here, shoot him, but don't do the girl until we call. She's still our insurance policy. Sid and I will follow Pete and take care of that end. As soon as I call, kill her." He stood up.

"You coming back here?" Paulie asked as he slid into the chair across from me.

"No. Just clean up the place, then head for Chicago." Dillman started for the door, then stopped and looked back at Paulie. "And Paulie—don't waste time. Kill her and get clear."

He turned and left, without even glancing at me. Sid silently followed his boss out the door. As he stepped past me, Marris started to say something, then stopped.

"Something the matter, big brother?" Paulie asked. He was leaning back in his chair, grinning.

Marris didn't say anything for a moment. He looked at me for a few seconds, whistling under his breath. Then he licked his lips and turned away. "I don't want to see you again, Paulie," he said over his shoulder. He left, slamming the door.

"Oh, you will, big brother, you will," Paulie said to the closed door. "Someday." He stood up and held the gun on me as he circled around, going over to lock the door. Then he went back to his chair, circling around the same way he had before. As if he was afraid I was going to jump him. I could have laughed, except I felt too sick and frightened.

"Now we wait," he said. "Don't try anything. The boss doesn't want me to kill you yet, but I don't have to kill you to stop you." He smiled at me, the same nasty smile I'd seen on his face before.

If time had passed slowly earlier, it now seemed to have stopped completely. I'm not even sure how long it was before I heard a car

183

stop outside. Paulie stood up and peered out the window.

"Donna?" It was Greg, calling to me from the parking lot. Paulie had a tight, triumphant grin on his face as pulled me to my feet. He held me by one arm, the gun pressed to my ribs, and shoved me over to the door.

"Answer him!" Paulie hissed in my ear, poking another bruise into my ribs. I didn't say anything, and he jabbed me again.

"Greg?" I hadn't wanted him to come; I'd wanted him to send the police. He hadn't understood my message. This was it: Greg was going to die, then Mom, then me. For the first time since that morning, I thought of Harry Leiberwitz. This must have been how he'd felt, when he knew he couldn't get away. Just before Paulie shot him.

Paulie reached past me and unlocked the door. He pushed it open and shoved me forward a step. "Tell him to come in," he whispered.

It was dark outside and I couldn't see Greg. But I wasn't going to invite him in to be killed. "Greg?" I took another step, filling my lungs to scream, to tell him to run for his life, when another voice yelled, *"Down!"*

Suddenly a hand reached around the door and grabbed me by the arm, pulling me onto my knees just as the whole world exploded in front of me.

For a moment I was the center of a tug-of-war as Paulie tried to pull me back inside and Greg pulled me out. Then Paulie swore and slammed the door. A moment later there was a tinkle of shattering glass as he broke the front window. That was followed by a shot, and I threw myself onto my stomach as something riffled my hair. The bullet missed me by only an inch. Greg lay beside me. There was another shot as he rolled over onto his knees. Then a barrage of shots was fired in front of us, aimed at the cottage. Greg pointed wildly to the corner of the cottage, about five feet behind me, and said, "That way!" I scrambled and rolled toward the corner, as Greg burst from a crouch like a sprinter, heading the opposite way, diving for the tail of our car in the driveway. He didn't make it.

I reached the corner just as Greg cried out, falling to the ground. He was still half a dozen steps from the car, unprotected in the parking lot. I choked off a scream as I realized he wasn't dead, he was still moving. But his left leg was bleeding heavily. He pulled himself forward on his elbows, then froze as a shot hit the dirt right in front of him.

In the sudden silence Paulie called out. "Try to get the girl and he's dead. Same thing if you move, punk. Now, let's see if we can talk reasonable about this."

185

A voice I didn't recognize called from in front, "Don't shoot. You got anyone else in there with you?"

Paulie said something, but I didn't catch it because someone touched me from behind. I gasped just as a voice said, "You okay, Miss White?" I turned around, tearing my eyes away from Greg. Detective Ed Johnston stood there, looking grim.

~ Thirteen ~

"Are you all right?" he asked me. "Were you hit?"

I stopped gaping at him and shook my head. "But Greg . . ."

He stuck his head cautiously around the end of the building and looked. "He's still alive. Don't know how much longer he'll stay that way, though. Who's inside, how many?"

"Just one. Paulie Marris." I swallowed tears. "H-he's the one who shot Mom, and he's killed others."

"Marris? Same as the marshal?"

"His younger brother. Inspector Marris and the others have gone after Mom. They're going to hijack the ambulance."

Johnston swore. "I'll have to radio the highway patrol for more men, then. We can't leave, not until this is settled. He can't get away, but if we rush him, the Florian kid'll get killed. He'll bleed to death anyway if we don't get him out of there soon."

He must have seen something in my face, dark as it was; or maybe I said something, I don't know.

"I'm sorry," he said, squeezing my shoulder. "He's a good kid, and that was pretty brave, his going up to the door like that. It was his idea."

In front the other cop called out something, and I heard Paulie answer, in the same tone of voice he'd used with Dillman. Johnston scowled.

"We can't wait much longer," he said. "McGill is a good man. He can keep Marris talking all night, but—I was hoping I could find a way in through the back here, but there's nothing."

My throat suddenly tight, I asked, "Do you have a flashlight? I know a way in."

He unclipped a metal flashlight from his belt. "Lead the way."

I ran to the back of the small tourist cottage, straining my shaky legs. The voices continued from out front, Paulie trying to make a deal, the cop playing for time. And Greg was lying there bleeding in the dirt. *Hang on*, I thought, *just*

He sat up and swung his legs down over the edge of the trap, being careful to miss the clothes rod. Then he sat there, gun in hand. I didn't know what he was waiting for, until I heard the sound of the voice outside, yelling something to Paulie.

As soon as Paulie started to answer, Johnston shifted forward and slid down through the trapdoor. I heard a thump as he landed, but it was muffled by Paulie's voice. I leaned over, staring down. Johnston glanced up at me and shook his head once, then brought his left hand up to grasp the gun along with his right. He kicked the door open the rest of the way and jumped at the same time, yelling, *"Freeze!"*

There might have been one second of silence, then the night exploded again with shots. As quickly as they started, they ended, leaving my ears ringing with the noise. I held my breath. Then the breath left me in a gasp as Johnston's voice called out, "All right, it's over." He sounded tired.

I scrambled around, dropping through the trapdoor and landing clumsily on my bad leg. I stumbled out into the room, which stank from the gunfire. Already the door was open, and people—some in uniforms, some not—had filled the room. Johnston turned to me as I came out and repeated, "It's over."

Paulie Marris lay on the floor by the window. He was dead.

I looked at his body for a moment, then I started to shake. Turning blindly away, I bumped into someone. "Easy," he muttered. It was Johnston.

"Greg. Is he . . ." I broke off. I was afraid to step to the door, afraid Greg would be lying dead in the dirt, his eyes as empty as Paulie's.

"Lost a lot of blood, but they've got a pressure bandage on it, and he should be okay once we get him to the hospital."

"The hospital! Mom—we've got to get there right away, before Marris gets Mom away from the hospital!"

Johnston froze for a moment. "All right, we won't wait for the ambulance. Let's get moving."

Within seconds we were on the road. In less than fifteen minutes the ambulance was supposed to pick up Mom. Greg insisted on coming with us, and Johnston didn't argue, since it would get him to the hospital faster. He was on the radio even before the unmarked squad car was out of the drive. A uniformed cop was behind the wheel, and Greg and I were in the back. He sat sideways, with his left leg up on the seat, and I had my arms around him. He kissed me as we pulled away from the Tour Rest Motel, leaving the lights and confusion behind. I just held on to him, shuddering.

"Donna, you're all right," he said. He repeated it several times.

"I'm fine," I said, which wasn't really true. Bruises, a bloody lip, what might be a concussion—but there wasn't time to worry about any of that. It could wait.

"Greg, your leg—how bad is it?" He was still pressing a wad of red cloth to it, cloth that had once been white. In the brief moment when the car's interior light had been on, I'd glimpsed his face. He had that waxy look Mom had after she'd been shot.

"I can't feel it right now," he said. "It's numb. I think the bone is broken. One of the cops touched it, and I almost passed out."

"I'm sorry," I whispered.

"Hey, now we'll both limp around for a while." He tried to smile. "It could have been worse."

"It could have been a *lot* worse," Johnston said from the front seat. "It's a good thing Greg managed to figure out what you meant, Donna. It didn't make any sense to me when he told me, but he kept insisting you were in danger from Marris, and, well, I had my own reasons to distrust the man." His voice trailed away, and I thought about Marris pulling me away from the hospital. He'd been trying to make Johnston look bad, which had made *him* look bad to the local cop.

"I told you, it was all in the play," Greg said. "Jonathan Brewster, the evil brother who's in disguise."

"Except the *real* evil brother was Paulie," I said. I closed my eyes for a moment, remembering. "Paulie was just as crazy as Jonathan is supposed to be. Only, in the play it's funny. Paulie wasn't."

"Killers usually aren't," Johnston agreed soberly.

"Anyway, I knew you meant there was something wrong with Marris," Greg said. "I almost missed it, you sounded so casual. For a moment, when you said it, I wondered who Jonathan was, like maybe he was someone we really knew. Then it hit me. As soon as I hung up, I called Detective Johnston, and, well, everything else happened."

"Everything else" including a shot leg. I hadn't told him yet that Paulie had been planning on killing him. Now I did, and I felt his body shivering as he realized just how big a risk he'd taken. It didn't matter if he'd known or not, though; he'd known it was a risk, and he'd gone ahead anyway. As far as I was concerned, Greg had earned a flock of medals whether he ever got any or not.

"There it is," Johnston said softly as we approached the hospital. I breathed in sharply as I saw what he meant. An ambulance was pulled up by the side entrance, its rear door swung wide open. All I could see was one man, near the front, probably the driver. It looked as if we'd made it in time.

"Pull into the parking lot," Johnston told the driver. He pointed to a spot about forty feet away from the ambulance. "That looks like a good place."

As the car stopped, Johnston turned around to speak to us. "You kids stay in the car. I'm going to see if we can handle this peacefully. Greg, we'll get you inside as soon as we can."

He got out and headed for the entrance, breaking into a jog as the door opened and a couple of paramedics pushed out a rolling gurney with a patient strapped to it. Mom. Another man in medical clothes followed, and in the rear were two men in suits. One of them was a stranger, but the other was Marris.

I rolled down my window so I could hear, and Greg slid over beside me. Johnston reached the group just as they got to the rear of the ambulance.

"Where are you taking Mrs. White?" Johnston said, his voice carrying clearly. "I thought I told you I wanted some answers first, Marris."

He sounded too tense, I thought. Marris would know something was wrong. But Marris's answer sounded the same, as if it were a continuation of their earlier fight over jurisdiction.

"And I told *you* you don't have any standing in this. It's a federal matter. There's been an attempt on this witness's life, and we're moving her to a more secure spot."

"Yeah, like a cemetery," Greg said under his breath.

I turned my head to say something to him and caught a glimpse of movement from the corner of my eye. For a split second what I saw made no sense at all; then the shape of the black sedan alongside us registered on my brain, and I screamed, "Get *down*!" as I grabbed Greg and pulled him sideways with me off the backseat of the car. We landed jammed between the front and back seats just as the side windows shattered above us. Even the noise of breaking glass didn't cover the sound of the shots.

Greg was squashed beneath me, struggling to push me off. I scrambled onto the seat just as the front door opened and our driver jumped out. He started running toward the back of the ambulance, pulling his gun as he ran, then dived to the ground. Two more shots came from the black car, which had now swung around in front of us, about twenty feet behind the ambulance. Mom's stretcher was still outside the ambulance, right behind the open door. One of the paramedics had been hit by the gunfire and lay on the ground beside the stretcher. I could see blood pouring down his arm. The other marshal was kneeling on the other side of the stretcher, gun in hand. Johnston was using the bulk of the ambulance as a shield between him and the black car. He also had his gun out, but he hadn't fired yet. It was easy to tell why: Mom was right in the line of fire. Marris had disappeared.

I didn't even hear the door beside me open. The nightmare in front of me had me so petrified, I doubt if I would have noticed any normal sound. But I noticed when Greg managed to pull himself behind the steering wheel. He fumbled with the gearshift, muttering, "Good, they left the keys."

"Greg, what are you *doing*?" I asked.

A single shot splintered the silence, off to one side.

"Keeping them from killing anyone else," he said. "Hang on!"

As though the single shot had been a signal, guns started going off on both sides. Greg started the engine with a roar that drowned out even the gunfire and threw the car into gear, then

197

floored it, aiming right for the side of the black car.

I don't think it took more than two seconds for us to cross the short gap, not enough time to build much speed. But it was enough. I heard a shout just before we hit, and I braced myself against the seat, preparing for impact. We slammed into the rear door and fender of the black car just as it started to move. The collision sent it spinning around, slapping into the side of the squad car.

The abrupt silence was broken only by the sounds of shattering glass and hissing metal. I pulled myself up. I hadn't had my seat belt on, and I wound up sprawled on the floor. Greg's nose was bleeding; I think he hit the steering wheel. The door beside Greg was yanked open, and I looked around through the haze of an intense headache. The cop who'd been driving earlier stood there.

"Sorry," Greg mumbled. He dabbed at his nose, then slid out, managing to balance himself against the side of the car. I crawled over to the driver's side and got out. On the other side Johnston and the marshal were hustling Sid and Dillman out of the pile of scrap metal that moments before had been an expensive car. The entire side had collapsed, springing the trunk and jamming the rear door. That was one vehicle that wasn't going to move again without a tow truck. I stared at the front of the squad car and winced. It wasn't going to get much farther than the black one would; it looked like an accordion.

I was having trouble hearing anything, between the gunshots and the crash and the sirens. I hadn't even noticed them before. Through the ringing I heard Johnston ask Greg, "Just what did you think you were doing?"

"I just thought—is Mrs. White okay? I mean Mrs. Aubrey?"

Johnston nodded, and the ringing in my ears sounded like a celebration. "She wasn't hit, if that's what you mean."

"That was what I meant to do, then," Greg said. He was dead white under the harsh parking-lot lights, but he managed a grin. "And it kept them from getting away. Maybe I should plan on being a stuntman instead of an actor." He turned and took one step toward me before his eyes rolled back in his head and he fainted, sliding down the side of the car. Johnston grabbed him before he dropped completely, easing him the rest of the way to the pavement.

"Shock," he said shortly. "He'll be okay, but he's going to spend some time in the hospital himself." He stood up. "Well, he's in the right place for it. *We need a medic!*" he shouted, waving his arms. One of the small group around the stretcher broke away and came toward us.

My eyes suddenly focused on the stretcher. Mom. Johnston said she was okay, but I wouldn't believe it until I saw for myself. I took a shaky step toward the ambulance, then another, and suddenly I was running, tears dripping down my face.

"She's fine," a familiar voice said. It was Dr. Harkness. I hadn't even seen him come out of the hospital. "All of my patients should be so lucky."

"I don't know about lucky. Getting mixed up in a crime, having to go on the run like we did, getting *shot* . . ."

"But she survived it." He checked one of the portable monitors that was hooked up to her. She hadn't opened her eyes, but that didn't surprise me, since I figured they'd sedate her for the trip. "Survived several attempts, in fact. And she's doing great. I'd call that lucky."

I reached for her free hand; there were tubes in the back of only one now. Lucky. Mom was alive, and so was I, and so was Greg. Compared to Harry Leiberwitz, I guessed we were. Or Mr. Peterson. An evening out watching a high-school play had gotten him killed. Even Paulie's luck had finally run out.

"Yeah, maybe we have been pretty lucky," I

said, squeezing Mom's hand gently.

"And maybe you'll keep on being lucky, if you do just like I say."

A rough hand grabbed me and pulled me back. Marris had vanished earlier during the gunfight, but now he had an arm like a steel belt around my shoulders, hugging me back against him. For a moment I tried to pry his arm away, but it was like trying to shift a bridge. Then I dropped my hands as I felt a feather-light touch on the hair at the side of my neck. Without turning my head, I knew it was a gun.

"Marris!" Johnston shouted. He and the marshal had turned around as soon as Marris spoke. They had handcuffs on Dillman and Sid, but now they all stopped moving.

"Pete, took you long enough to get here," Dillman said. He started toward us. "Get the keys to these damned cuffs and let's get out of here."

Dillman stopped as the gun moved away from my neck and pointed past my ear. I didn't dare turn my head, but I could see the end of it from the corner of my eye.

"You aren't going anyplace," Marris said. "We're through, Dillman. All I want is the keys to the ambulance. Who's got them?"

"Why, you . . ." Dillman took another step toward us, his face twisting in fury, but Johnston pulled him back. Beside Johnston, the other marshal furiously glared at Marris. I didn't see him move, but Marris must have read something else in his expression, because the gun came back around, barely brushing my hair.

"I haven't killed anyone yet," he said, his voice so low it almost didn't carry across to the others. "They have, not me. I don't want to start now, but I will if you force me to. Now give me the keys! *Now!*"

"Do as he says," Johnston said. Dr. Harkness bent over Mom suddenly, and I saw her eyes flicker open. *Don't wake up now, Mom,* I thought. *Not now.*

A woman dressed in the ambulance company's uniform stepped forward, keys dangling from her outstretched hand. She stopped several paces away.

"Hand them to me carefully," Marris said. She stepped forward slowly until he could grab the keys. "Now back away slowly." She did, and Marris started to back away as well, dragging me with him. "Everyone stay where you are," he ordered. His arm had shifted up until it was in a choke hold across my neck. I couldn't move. I almost couldn't breathe. I pried again at his arm, but it was hopeless. Suddenly the death grip slackened. I wheezed, drawing air into my lungs in ragged gasps; then he pulled me around.

Marris stared at me, his expression colder than any his brother had ever worn. For a moment I thought he intended to shoot, and my knees turned to rubber. Then he brought both hands up and shoved me backward, so hard, I stumbled several feet before landing flat on my backside. Before I hit the ground, he slammed the door and peeled out in the ambulance.

Johnston and the other marshal came running across to me and helped me to my feet. "We'll get him," the marshal said. I didn't know if he was talking to me or to himself, but he sounded determined. He turned abruptly and left, running over to the squad car. Johnston gave me his arm to lean on, and we followed more slowly. Ahead paramedics were working on Greg again, and they wheeled him into the hospital before we had gone more than half the distance.

Dillman and Sid were being led to another squad car. Before he climbed in, Dillman stopped and looked across at me. "I was right, Miss Aubrey. You're more trouble than you're worth." Then he climbed in, and one of the cops shut the door.

We crossed over to the gurney. Mom's eyes were open. I smiled and reached for her hand. "It's all right, Mom. I'm here, and everything's going to be all right. It's all over. At last it's all over."

203

~ Fourteen ~

Nine months had passed since that terrible week. I was home again, back in Norwell on a weekend trip from college. We had left the program for good in October. After that Mom and I had tried to go back to Lakewood Heights, but oddly enough, we didn't fit in anymore. Mom's job had vanished with Dillman Brothers, and most of Mom's old friends acted embarrassed, as though she'd done something wrong herself. The publicity had ruined our life there. Too much had happened since then, and there were too many memories in the old house. Memories of pain.

Mom might not have gotten to know many people in Norwell, but she had made a few friends. Especially the Cottinghams, Tina's folks.

By Christmas we had decided to move back to Illinois. Mom's boss in Norwell wanted her back, and even though the job didn't pay as much as what she'd once made at Dillman's, she had enjoyed working there. I'd already been accepted at the University of Illinois. So the previous month, at the beginning of second semester, Mom had returned to Norwell, and I had moved into a dorm room in Urbana.

I got home most weekends, with Urbana less than an hour's drive from Norwell. I'd gone over to Greenmoor right after I started school and looked up Mrs. Beal. I told her the whole story; I figured she'd earned the right to hear it. She'd gotten to know Mom since then, and they had become friends.

But Mom wasn't home this weekend. She'd had to go back east for what they promised would be the last time, tying up loose ends on the Pete Marris investigation. I'd come home anyway, and when I'd bumped into Miss Ahrens downtown, I'd gotten her to let me into the auditorium while she caught up on paperwork in her classroom. Now I sat in one of the musty old seats out front, looking up at the empty stage and remembering.

I've never really been the sort to spend a lot of time reminiscing, but sometimes the past doesn't give you much choice. I was eager for the case to be closed, so I could get on with my life. But the memories wouldn't leave me alone as long as there were still unanswered questions about what had happened.

The rest of that terrible night was a blur. They took Greg into surgery right away for his leg; I didn't get to see him again until graduation. All they did for me was rebandage my thigh, X-ray my skull to check for concussion, and give me a bed for the night. I spent the night there, officially "under observation" but really just crashing. I slept twelve hours.

Some unanswered questions were answered over the next few weeks. But the biggest one remained open: Marris. At first everyone expected him to be caught within a few minutes—then within a few hours, then a few days. He never was. He'd driven less than a half mile in that ambulance, ditching it inside an abandoned garage and stealing a car, which he exchanged for another stolen car a few miles later. I guess it helps when you're running from the law to know all the tricks that the law knows.

I got cross-examined about him by what seemed like every U.S. marshal in the service. Marris was an embarrassment to them, the first marshal to go bad. From what they told Mom, he'd vanished completely, and they'd run out of leads.

Everything else had sorted itself out gradually. There was some trouble about the squad car, of course. Greg had really done a number on it, and I think there was some talk about making him pay for it, but the subject was dropped once the full story came out, including the way he'd risked his life at the door of the motel room. I doubt if his father will ever trust him behind the wheel again, though. Totaling two cars in one weekend is a little extreme.

Thinking of Greg made me wonder where he was that weekend. The marshals had pulled us out of Norwell the following day. Graduation had been a few weeks later, and Mom talked the marshals into letting me take part. They insisted on full protection, so there were almost as many marshals there as graduating seniors. Anyway, I did get my diploma, a real one, from Norwell High, with my real name on it. Greg was in a wheelchair for his, with plaster clear up to his hip. The audience cheered both of us, which I think embarrassed him as much as it did me. I gave him a hard time about that—Greg Florian not knowing how to handle an ovation.

After that Greg and I kept in touch through a mail drop the program set up, even while they had us back in that fortress in Washington. But except for graduation, we didn't see each other until Mom and I moved back to Norwell in

December. It was the best Christmas we'd had since Dad died.

Even though Greg and I were still close friends, we weren't a couple anymore. He was enrolled in the theater-arts program at Millikin University in Decatur, about forty miles away from the University of Illinois.

He told me he'd never forget that when he grabbed Paulie's arm the night of the play, he saved my mother's life at the cost of Mr. Peterson's. If Greg hadn't been there, Mom would have died, and his neighbor would have lived. Greg didn't intend to hurt Mr. Peterson, and he doesn't regret saving Mom, but still, it's something he has to live with. And he still has a limp. We'll always be good friends; that wild run of ours will be a bond between us forever. But life doesn't usually come with happy-ever-after endings.

I got up and headed down the aisle to the stage. The curtain was open, but without the work lights it was gloomy and felt almost sad. Memories. Over in the wings I saw a painted piece of the set that we'd used for *Arsenic and Old Lace*. I doubt if I'll ever be able to watch that play again.

At odd times since we'd left the program, I'd felt as if someone were watching me. I didn't like walking across campus at night, and I'd gotten in the habit of staying with other people most of the time. It was mostly my own imagination, I figured. But there was one loose end. I would have slept better if they had caught Marris. As it was, I still jumped at shadows.

Anyway, we left the program in mid-October, after Dillman had been sentenced. It will be ironic if he winds up in the witness-protection program someday, but I have a hunch he will. At any rate, he'll know better when they tell him how foolproof it is. We were a big embarrassment to them, the first witnesses to be hurt while covered by the program, by the first marshal to go bad. Mom says they'll probably decide that our story doesn't count, since I *did* break the rules by joining the play without clearance and Marris *did* go bad. Makes me wonder how many other cases haven't counted.

Of course, Marris had been a fluke, a disaster waiting to happen. He'd had a clean record, but no one in the marshal service had ever known about his kid brother, the one who'd disappeared years before. The one who had turned into a professional hit man.

Dillman told the marshals all about it. When we disappeared after Harry was killed, Dillman found out we were in the program. A security leak gave him Marris's name. It was an unusual name, and when Dillman met Paulie, he wondered about it. He said when he asked Paulie about it, Paulie thought it was the funniest thing he'd heard in his life. He hadn't known his older brother was a marshal.

The stage smelled of dust and old paint. Like most high schools, Norwell uses the same props again and again. Over to one side of the stage was the fancy little round table we'd used in the play. If I poked around, I'd probably be able to find one of the decanters we'd used for our "elderberry wine." I was taking a couple of drama classes at the U of I, even though I'm majoring in French. I'll probably always enjoy acting, but I can see how theaters get a reputation for being haunted. An empty stage is full of ghosts.

I gave a tug on the curtain rope, and it moved easily, shutting the curtains partway. The backstage area looked even gloomier, with the only light being the single emergency bulb over the exit. It was getting late; I should go find Miss Ahrens and let her lock up. I started toward the gap in the curtains when I heard a creak from the auditorium.

"Miss Ahrens?" I called. "I'm backstage. Everything's just the way I remember it. You've used that main flat again, I see. . . ."

I expected to hear Miss Ahrens's cheerful voice answering me, but there was silence. I stepped back a pace, suddenly nervous.

"Miss Ahrens?"

There was no answer, only an auditorium full of silence. Then the silence was broken by a sound I recognized immediately. It was a sort of hissing whistle. The noise Inspector Pete Marris made.

My heart was pounding harder than it had pounded since that night. I pulled back, hiding myself in the folds of the curtain. I wished I hadn't called out like that. He knew I was still in here.

The breathy little whistle drew closer; then I heard the soft creak of the wooden steps that led up to the stage. I froze, and there was dead silence for a moment. He must have realized that I'd heard him.

"I've been watching you for a long time," his voice called out to me softly. "Do you know who this is, Donna?"

I shivered. Maybe it hadn't been my imagination, all those times I'd felt as if someone was behind me. I shifted my head about a half inch, to a gap in the curtain folds. He stood center stage, lit by the single emergency light and the trickle of light from the front. I don't know if I would have recognized him by sight alone. Instead of the super-clean-cut U.S. marshal I remembered, he looked like a bum. His hair was long and shaggy, and he had a scruffy beard and clothes that looked as if he'd fished them out of a trash barrel. He seemed to have lost about forty pounds, and he looked *hungry*. Life on the wrong side of the law had been rough on him, obviously.

He turned around slowly, trying to spot me, and my breath caught in my throat as I saw what I'd missed the first time. In his right hand, held low and to the side, he had a long-bladed knife that gleamed in the dim light.

"Come on, Donna, it's gone on long enough now. Come out and let's get this finished." He turned again.

Maybe being on the run had caused him to snap; maybe it was his brother's death. But he sounded crazier than Paulie ever had. I couldn't hold my breath any longer and let it out softly, hoping the heavy velvet drapes would muffle the sound.

Marris made another complete turn. Then he straightened up, facing me.

"There you are," he said. His voice was as casual as if nothing had ever happened. He came at me in a rush.

But by that time I was moving, pushing my way back through the curtains. I ran back to the emergency exit, but it was locked tight. Marris had slashed at the curtains, and it took him a few moments to get himself and the knife untangled; but as soon as he did, he turned toward me.

"All right, Donna," he said, walking slowly toward me. He took another step, and I inched to my left, trying to get out of the corner.

"Inspector, *why?*" I asked. "I didn't do anything."

"My little brother is dead because of you, Donna. And I'm not Inspector Marris anymore." He moved again and so did I, easing over to the stack of flats leaning against the back wall. "I'm just Pete now. Paulie's big brother."

"I didn't shoot him. Johnston did!" As I spoke, I grabbed the side of a flat and shoved it. The rickety construction of laths and painted canvas fell forward toward Marris, and I jumped the other way, trying to dodge around him. If I could get to the front of the auditorium, I thought, I'd be able to get away. He ducked back from the solid-looking wall as it fell on him, and it settled to the stage with a soft thump. But he was still between me and the front of the stage.

"You set him up for it," Marris said softly. I almost choked on the irony; he'd set Mom and me both up in the first place. "I should have killed you when I had a chance that night."

Suddenly I darted to the side, running across the fallen flat. The canvas tore beneath me, and I nearly tripped. Marris moved around the end, reaching the other side almost at the same time I did. He was still between me and the front of the stage.

I didn't bother trying to talk now. I just kept inching over as he closed on me. I measured the distance with my eyes as I moved. If I could get him far enough over to one side, I might be able to get past him. Once I got off the stage, I was sure I could outrun him.

I'd been angling toward the small round table that had been left in the wings. It was a solid piece of furniture that someone had donated to the Drama Department years before. Marris had closed in by this point to within twelve feet. There wouldn't be another chance.

I grabbed the table and threw it at him, running to the side as I did. He let out a yell and raised his arms to fend it off, and I cut for the edge of the stage. The table wasn't big enough or heavy enough to knock him down, but it was enough to distract him just for a moment. I raced forward, jumping into the black of the pit in front of the apron without pausing. I landed off balance and went down on one knee. As I scrambled to my feet, I looked back. Marris was almost to the front of the stage. I ran to the side aisle and started up when he yelled again. I turned my head just in time to see him falling over the edge as he tripped on a coil of cable someone had left on stage.

He made a funny sound as he landed, halfway between a groan and a scream. I hesitated. He got to his feet, took a single step toward me, then collapsed onto his knees, then his side. Even in the dim lights from the aisles, I could see the darkness of blood spreading along his side.

Then the room was no longer dim, as Miss Ahrens came running in and turned on all the houselights. I ran toward her, babbling out some jumbled version of what had happened, and we waited there by the door to the auditorium for several long minutes. There was no sound from the stage area. After a time that seemed years long, we went down the aisle.

Marris lay in a crumpled heap, the side of his shirt soaked with blood from the knife in his side. He'd landed on it when he fell off the stage. He was dead.

Slowly, we left the auditorium. After we called the police, I'd call Mom and tell her that, at last, it really was all over.

Here's a sneak preview of a terrifying new series by
Cynthia Blair

Dark Moon Legacy

Out on the edge of Overlook, an air of desolation hung as thick as the mist that blanketed the forest. The late-afternoon sun was barely visible against the gray sky as Miranda struggled to maneuver her bike over the narrow, pitted dirt road.

Winding Way was treacherous, an endless path of sharp turns and unexpected twists that snaked up into the hills. All around were rotted fences, jutting out from fields of weeds. Miranda hadn't been on this road since she was a child, when she and her friends used to head out on their bikes in search of adventure. She was dismayed over its state of disrepair. Yet what struck her most was the silence. Nothing, not even birds, seemed to dwell here on the outskirts of town.

But she had to see Garth. The memorial service, Mrs. Swensen's sharp words, the terrible insinuations of Corinne and Selina . . . it had all been too much for her to bear alone. By the time the final bell rang, her desire to be with Garth had grown to a desperate longing—but she'd had no idea where to find him. She stopped in at the library, hoping that she'd see him there. He spent a lot of time doing research, so someone there might even know where he lived.

"Now, let me see," Ms. Wallace, the library clerk, had said. She'd shuffled through a box of file cards, peering through the eyeglasses she wore on a chain around her neck. "He did apply for a card recently, so I should have . . . Oh, yes, here it is. Garth Gautier . . . Winding Way."

Ms. Wallace frowned. "Hmmm. The only house I know of on Winding Way is that dilapidated old estate. What is it called? Cedar Crest?"

Miranda was startled. "Garth lives at Cedar Crest?"

Ms. Wallace shook her head. "There must be some mistake. Nobody's inhabited that old eyesore for years. I'm surprised the Board of Health hasn't had it leveled by now."

"Thanks anyway." Miranda was already halfway out the door. Now, even as she pedaled around a bend in the road and caught sight of the old house, she couldn't believe Garth really lived here. She felt sure she had come all this way for nothing.

Miranda gazed up at Cedar Crest. It had always reminded her of a European castle, with its simple lines and stark landscaping. It was an elegant, L-shaped building made of pale gray stones. A tall tower joined the two wings, and along one side ran a row of French doors that opened onto the garden.

It had undoubtedly been a showplace at one time. Now, after decades of neglect, there was something forbidding about the mansion. Even in the bright afternoon light, it was shrouded in shadow. The darkened windows resembled dozens of unseeing eyes. Miranda shivered.

She leaned her bicycle against a tree and cautiously made her way toward the front door. Up close, she could see that the house was in a terrible state of decay. Many of the stones were pitted or even disintegrating. The brick path leading from the circular driveway to the front door was overgrown with weeds. She wondered if the crumbling steps would support her weight.

Miranda had to agree with Mrs. Wallace— Garth couldn't possibly live here. Still, it was the only address she had. Determined to find out, Miranda reached for the heavy brass knocker.

She was as surprised to see Garth appear at the door as he looked to see her.

"Miranda!" he said. "What are you doing here?"

"Can I come in?"

He hesitated for a moment, as if deciding, then stepped aside to let her in.

Relieved, Miranda walked into the foyer. It took a few seconds for her eyes to adjust to the darkness within. She found herself in a huge entryway. It ended at a dramatic marble staircase edged with an intricately carved wooden banister. On either side of her were cavernous rooms.

Miranda could tell that the rooms had once been elegant. Now they contained barely any furniture, the few pieces that remained obvious casualties of time. There were piles of rubble pushed into corners. Paint was peeling, decorative trim faded. And everywhere there were shadows, as if there were not enough light in the entire world to bring this place back to life.

"You shouldn't have come," Garth said woodenly. He was standing behind her as she surveyed the decrepit castle that was his home.

Miranda quickly forgot all about her bizarre surroundings. "I had to see you," she explained, turning to him.

"You don't belong here," he said in the same monotone.

"Oh, Garth, just hold me!" Unable to believe his coldness was sincere, she wrapped her arms around him and gazed up into his eyes, searching for the warmth and acceptance she craved. She desperately needed him to tell her she wasn't alone.

It seemed like an eternity before he finally clasped his arms around her, drawing her close. Miranda collapsed against his powerful chest, reveling in the sense of safety, of security, that she had yearned for.

It was like coming home.

She raised her face to his. The intensity in his blue eyes created a stirring deep inside her. Then he leaned forward, pressing his parted lips against hers. Gently at first, tentatively, as if he were asking a question. But his kiss quickly grew more ardent. Miranda eagerly gave in to it. Reaching up, she encircled his neck with her arms, her body melting against his.

Finally he drew back, nuzzling her neck. "My sweet, sweet Miranda," he whispered, his breath hot against her skin.

"Hold me," she pleaded, clinging to him. "Don't ever let go."

He grasped her even more tightly. "Oh, Miranda, what have they done to you?"

In a halting voice she told him everything. All about the memorial service for Andy Swensen. His mother's reaction to her expression of sympathy. The insensitivity of Corinne and Selina. Even her own self-doubts, her suspicion that, in some way she couldn't explain, she'd had something to do with Andy's death.

"Poor Miranda." Garth embraced her in his muscular arms, holding her as if he were desperate to infuse her with some of his own strength. "Let's forget all that for now. Let's just appreciate how wonderful it is to be together."

He took her gently by the hand and led her through the house. Miranda was breathless as she took it all in. Room after room, each more beautiful, more ornate than the last . . . all of them slipping into ruin as if they'd been cursed.

Out back was a garden. Like the rest of the house, it had obviously been lovely once. Now it was covered with weeds, the meandering paths barely visible through the stubby grass that pushed its way through. Still, Miranda could make out what had once been a rose garden, picturing it in her mind as it must have looked in late spring, alive with pink and red and yellow buds. In one corner was a fish pond, an oddly shaped pool of water that was now murky and covered with algae. Off in the distance was a maze, fashioned from shrubs that over time had become oddly misshapen. Despite its state of decline, Miranda was awestruck, and even a bit intimidated, by its grandeur.

"What a magical place!" she breathed, sinking onto a crumbling concrete bench. "How did you come to live here?"

"My family owns this estate. My grandfather built it after he made a fortune in the lumber industry." Garth glanced around with a rueful smile. "This was his reward."

"Where is he now?"

"He died a long time ago. My father had already established himself up in Portland, so he just closed it up. When I had to get out . . . when I decided to leave Portland, I came down here and opened the place up."

"Isn't it lonely, living here by yourself?" Miranda asked with concern.

A look of pain crossed Garth's face. In an even voice, he told her, "I've been alone my whole life."

They sat for a long time, hands locked together, allowing the peacefulness of the garden to settle over them. Miranda found herself telling him much of what was in her heart—the pain, the confusion, even the hope. Once again she was surprised by how easy it was being with him. Talking to him. Trusting him. Gradually a sense of peace returned.

"Let's go inside," he suggested as the sky grew darker and the gentle spring breezes became stronger. He led her back into the house, this time going off in a different direction.

They ended up in the ballroom. Miranda let out a gasp. What a magnificent room! Her eyes traveled upward, taking in the hand-carved running frieze joining the walls to the ceiling, the elaborate gold-leaf trim, the ornate cornices above the windows.

"Oh, Garth, it's gorgeous," she cried, taking his arm. "This entire house is like something out of a dream. Wouldn't it be wonderful if we could bring it alive again? We could make it just as beautiful as it was when your grandfather first built it."

She grew more excited as she imagined it. "I could work in the garden—I'll bet I could get it back into terrific shape in a single summer. And inside, we could paint and make repairs. . . ." She cast a sidelong glance at Garth, anxious to see if he was going along with her fantasy. Instead, the look on his face frightened her.

"What is it, Garth?"

"It's hearing you talk like that."

Miranda bit her lip. "I'm sorry. I didn't mean—"

"Don't you see, Miranda?" he cried. "Don't you know that's what I want too? For us to be together here? More than anything. I'd give anything if we could make it happen!"

She recoiled, taken aback by the force of his words. "Why can't we?"

"We can't see each other anymore. You must accept that."

"But I love you," she said in a quiet voice. "And . . . and I want to stay with you."

She took a step forward, her eyes locked on his, her arms held slightly toward him. With her entire body she was asking a question. Her breaths were short and quick, her chest heaving as she waited for his answer.

But instead of feeling him melt against her the way she'd hoped, she saw his muscles tense.

"No, Miranda. Don't."

"But I do love you! I can't just stop. I—I don't want to stop!"

Garth buried his face in his hands. He paced about the room, so agitated it seemed as though some other spirit had taken him over. "I was afraid of this. I tried to stop it, I thought I could control it—"

"Garth, what is it?" Miranda was confused. "Why is it wrong for me to love you? Why would I ever want to stop feeling the most wonderful feeling I've ever—"

"You don't understand." As he turned to face her, she expected to see anger in his blue eyes.

Instead, she saw desperation. "I'm not what you think I am."

"But, Garth—"

"Go away, Miranda," he pleaded. "Before it's too late."

She reached up and gently placed her hand against his cheek. "It's already too late."

He moved her hand away. "Miranda, there are things about me you don't know."

"Then tell me," she pleaded. "I want to know. I want to know everything about you."

"You couldn't possibly understand—"

"I understand how I feel. I understand, for the first time in my life, what it means to love."

She took a few more steps toward him, but he drew back. He was running away from her again. He didn't want her. He knew how she felt—maybe even felt that way too, at least a little—yet he was choosing to give her up.

Suddenly a new feeling washed over her. She could feel her frustration escalating into anger.

"You're absolutely right, Garth," Miranda said. "I *don't* understand. I see that there could be something special, something wonderful between us. There already is—or at least I thought there was. But for some reason you're afraid of it. You're turning your back on it."

"Listen to me, Miranda! It's not what you think!"

"I don't know what to think. But there's one thing I do know. And that's that you're sending me

225

away. All right; I'll go. It's not as if you're the only boy in the world who could possibly care for me."

"What are you talking about?"

A surge of power was rushing through her. She felt it was dangerous . . . yet she was already out of control, unable to stop it. "There's someone else. Someone who pours out his heart to me in beautiful love poems. Someone who's not afraid of my love!"

She whirled around, racing toward the door of the ballroom. As she did, she heard him say her name one more time.

"Miranda!" It came out like a groan, a desperate plea.

She didn't turn back. Instead, she rushed outside into the late afternoon. The air was tinged with iciness. The approaching dusk was already painting the sky with striking reds and oranges, the towering trees darkening against the colorful backdrop.

As always, the dramatic landscape reminded her that she was but one small part of a universe so great and so powerful that it was impossible to fathom. But her own pain was so wrenching, her feelings of loss so great, her hopelessness so devastating, that this time there was no comfort even in that thought.

Once again the moon was full.

The autumn night was biting, winter's icy fingers already gripping the forest.

Tonight, he was not part of the night.

Instead, he gazed out the window, narrow panes crisscrossed with iron bars.

He had imprisoned himself purposely. Earlier that evening, he had waited inside Cedar Crest, agonizing over his fate . . . wondering if perhaps he could alter it.

He knew that the change would come upon him tonight. That once again the beast would be unable to resist its evil nature. Yet he was determined to fight the desire to seek out human flesh. And so when night began to fall, he had descended into the depths of Cedar Crest, where his only weapon against total blackness was a single hurricane lamp. He watched as its pale flame cast long shadows upon the crumbling stone steps and the narrow twisting hallways.

Down in the cellar, among the thick cobwebs, nestled between the now-empty wine cellar and the abandoned storage areas, was a small room. He had been inside only once, puzzling over its purpose.

Now he understood.

It was a prison of sorts, a cell in which someone—or something—could be locked away, unable to cause harm. The only window was barred. The door was thick wood, so warped that it was wedged firmly into the concrete frame.

The lock was on the outside.

He wasn't sure his plan would work, but he had to try. If only this room could contain him while the moon was full! If only it could enforce a control that he himself lacked.

If only this room would keep the werewolf from killing again.

When the moon began to rise, he had come inside, pushing hard against the door, confident that even the strongest animal would be unable to find a way of getting past it.

Now he waited.

Staring out the window, he watched the moon rise, and felt the change begin. It started with a tingling sensation that electrified his skin. His jaw lengthened, his muscles swelled, fine golden hairs sprouted everywhere. He watched with great curiosity, anxious to see how the beast would react.

Gradually the boy's awareness faded. Once again the beast emerged.

At first it was confused. It blinked, unable to comprehend the four gray walls that surrounded it, containing it inside such a small space.

It grew more agitated as it paced, sniffing the walls, searching for a means of escape. It yearned to test its muscles to the limit, to race through the forest. Its senses were as sharp as always, its nostrils flaring as it tried to pick out anything familiar, its ears pricked in an attempt at discovering what this place was.

And then, the rage.

Never before had the beast been contained. Never before had its instinctive drive to roam freely through the forest been restrained. Never before had its urge to hunt been crushed.

The beast raised its head to release an agonized howl of defeat.

Then it heard the voices.

"Are you sure about this, Corinne?"

"What are you, Paul, chicken?"

Two boys. They spoke in whispers, their voices edged with fear. The beast froze, its senses even more alert than before.

"Come on, Tommy. Don't back out on us now. You promised, remember?"

A girl, this time.

"Besides, it's only a practical joke. Paul's idea about shooting off firecrackers was a brainstorm."

"Yeah, but you'd better keep your voice down, Corinne. Otherwise the only surprise around here is gonna be Miranda's boyfriend coming after us with a baseball bat."

The beast heard their words without understanding them. What it did understand was that the three voices were right outside the basement window, coming closer every second.

The urge to hunt was overwhelming.

"How are we supposed to get in?" demanded one of the boys. "The front door's locked."

"Are you guys for real?" The girl's tone was one of exasperation. "We'll break in through the basement. There's probably a door somewhere."

There was a long silence. "I don't know, Corinne," said one of the boys. "That's breaking

229

and entering. Not exactly the same thing as a practical joke."

"You are afraid, aren't you? Well, who needs you? I can do this myself."

"Let's go back, Corinne." The boy sounded even more afraid than before. "Maybe this wasn't such a good idea, after all."

"You go. I can manage. Give me that flashlight."

The beast watched through the window, taking care to stay in the shadows. Every muscle was tense. It longed to strike out, to break through the glass. Yet something inside told it to hold back—to hide in the darkness and wait.

The three of them argued some more, gradually moving out of the beast's range. Once again it began its agitated pacing. It leaped up against the cold stone walls, its head nearly reaching the ceiling. There was no way out. Anxiously it circled the small space, desperate to escape. And then it froze.

It heard a noise.

It pointed its ears upward. Someone was rattling the rotted wooden door at the end of the corridor.

From the scent, the beast knew it was the girl.

And then she was inside the house.

"I knew it," she muttered. "An old wreck like this is bound to be easy to get into. Now all I need is a place to light these stupid firecrackers."

The beast stood perfectly still. It lurked in the

230

shadowy space next to the door, prepared to pounce. Its nose twitched as the scent of the girl grew stronger.

She was moving closer.

And then, "Are you nuts, Corinne? Let's get out of here!"

One of the boys had come back.

"Look, Paul. I've come this far—"

"If you get caught, you're dead! Come on! It's not worth it."

"Oh, all right. You go ahead with Tommy. I'll catch up with you in a minute."

"Do what you want, but Tommy and I are outta here."

Her scent was growing weaker. She was moving away. The beast relaxed its stance, lying on the cold stone floor in defeat. It could hear her moving down the corridor uncertainly.

The footsteps stopped. For a long time, there was silence. The beast waited, ears pricked, not yet ready to give up.

And then the sound resumed, this time taking a different direction. Suddenly her scent flooded the room. She was pushing against the door.

Instantly the beast was poised. With a great creaking sound, the wooden door moved. In the dim light it saw her silhouette in the doorway.

She paused, blinking. And then, catching sight of the huge form crouching before her, she let out a piercing scream. She turned and ran, racing through the winding corridor. The beast followed. Its massive form was an encumbrance here in the narrow hallways, its movements slowed down by the slippery floor, the unexpected turns, the unfamiliar space in which even its keen senses could not help it find its way.

And then it was outdoors. The girl was rushing toward the woods, her gasping breaths filled with fear. The beast raced after her, loping across the fields, its urge to hunt stronger than ever.

Finally it reached the forest. Out here, no living creature could match the beast's speed. None could match its power.

None could match its determination.

Easily it reached the girl, catching up with her in a small clearing. She turned, a look of horror on her face, too terrified even to scream.

A glorious feeling of release washed over the beast. It stood poised for only a moment. And then it pounced, meeting with little resistance as it shoved its victim to the ground.

☎
1 (800) I LUV BKS!

If you'd like to hear more about your
favorite young adult novels and writers . . .
OR
If you'd like to tell us what you thought
of this book or other books
you've recently read . . .

CALL US at 1(800) I LUV BKS
[1(800)458-8257]

You'll hear a new message about books and
other interesting subjects each month.

**The call is free to you, but please get
your parents' permission first.**